This book is dedicated to my mother, the very beautiful Janice Williams. From day one, you've been my biggest supporter. From the numerous sales you've made to the different storyline ideas, all the way down to the constructive criticism—you've always had my back. No amount of words can explain how much you mean to me. You are indeed my best friend, and I love you beyond words. I am so blessed that God chose you to be my mother.

Contents

Dedication · 1

Buried Secrets: An Urban Novella · 5

Emera · 6

Emera · 12

Emera · 18

Emera · 22

Emera · 26

Emera · 33

Emera · 38

Emera · 41

Emera · 50

Emera · 55

Emera · 61

Emera · 72

Rocco · 75

Emera · 82

Rocco · 88

Emera · 92

Rocco · 97

Emera · 102

Rocco 107

Emera 114

Rocco 121

Emera 127

Rocco 132

Emera 143

Rocco 148

Emera 152

Epilogue 157

Buried Secrets: An Urban Novella

By N.L. Hudson

<h1 style="text-align:center">Emera</h1>

Ever since I was younger, I knew my life was destined to be fucked up. My mom was a crack whore who used our tiny, one-bedroom apartment to turn tricks. Her ass didn't give a damn if I was right there in the next room. All she cared about was the little forty dollars she got for spreading her legs. Then she had all kinds of men coming into our spot—dope boys, the mailman, businessmen, other crackheads; hell, even the landlord came through to get him a piece.

Night after night, I was forced to lay awake, listening to that old bed squeak. There were times when I wouldn't get any rest and would end up oversleeping for school. Whenever that happened, I got the brakes beat off my ass. Mama said if I wasn't for me trying to be nosy, I would hear my alarm. That bitch had to be batshit crazy. How the hell was I supposed to sleep throughout that commotion?

As far as my daddy went, his ass wasn't better. He was a married man that had cheated on his wife with my mama. The only time he acknowledged me was when we were alone. If I ever saw him out with his wife, he pretended to not know me. It was hard to deal with initially, but after a while, I just stopped giving a fuck.

"Emera, is that you?" Vladir asked, bringing me out of my thoughts.

"It's me. I need to talk to you right quick."

"What are you doing here this late? Did I forget to pay you?"

"Nah. It's about my mama."

"Come in. I'll put these things away, and then you can tell me about it."

Vladir was one of my mom's old Johns. He was a tall, white guy with chiseled features and baby-blue eyes. The first time I saw him, I thought he was cute for a white boy. Unlike those other men, Vladir was actually kind to me. He knew my mama was doing me dirty, so he always brought me food whenever he came through. He'd also given me a job to clean his place, even though it didn't need it.

"What's going on, Emera?" Vladir asked as soon as he sat down.

"Um." I wrung my wrist, glancing around.

"Are you going to tell me what's wrong, or am I gonna have to guess?" He half grinned.

Vladir had such a gentle smile. I knew for a fact that he genuinely cared about me. It wasn't in a creepy way either. It was almost as if I was like a daughter to him.

"Um," I repeated.

"It's okay. You can talk to me. Is she hitting you again?"

"No. It's not that…"

"Okay, so what it is. Don't be scared to talk to me. You know I'll keep you safe."

"She um…"

"Did one of her men try to mess with you?" Vladir's calm demeanor suddenly turned to one of rage.

Before I could reply, the front door flew open and scared

the shit out of me. Two men barged in waving pistols. One was tall with a brown complexion and a slim build. The snapback Chicago Bulls hat that was pulled low over his eyes made it hard for me to see his face. The other guy was of average height, had a stocky build, and was my complexion.

"You know what the fuck this is!" the brown skin guy told Vladir.

"Are you sure you wanna do this? I don't think you really know who you're dealing with!" Vladir piped.

The guy chuckled and slapped Vladir with the gun. "My nigga, do you realize who you dealing with? I will merk yo' bitch ass right here!"

Vladir shot him a sinister look. "You won't get away with this."

"Whatever, muthafucka. Yo, nigga, come tie him up." The guy instructed the other one. He then turned to me. "Aye, is this yo' nigga?"

"No. He's my friend," I whispered.

The man walked over and stuck the gun in my face. "Bitch, quit lying. I know he tappin' that young ass. How much he payin' you?"

"I just told you that we ain't fuckin!"

"Come with me," he ordered.

"Why?"

"Because I fuckin' said so! Get yo' raggedy ass up!" he barked.

I shot my eyes at Vladir. "Go ahead. He's not going to hurt you. I'll make sure of it."

The guy stomped back over and smashed Vladir in the

head with the pistol. "How the fuck you know what I'ma do? I'll kill you and this bitch right here! Keep talkin' shit!"

Vladir held his head as blood seeped through his fingers.

"Let's go, bitch! I ain't got all day!"

Reluctantly, I stood up and followed him out of the room. As soon as we hit the top stair of the mini-mansion, I stopped walking.

"What's the problem?" he asked.

"What the fuck was that down there, Shark? Why you stick that gun in my face and call me out my name?"

Shark is my man and had been for the past six months. I met him at the pool hall when me and my girls were hanging out.

"Relax. I had to make it look good. It's all a part of the plan." He leaned in and tried to kiss me, but I pushed his ass back.

"Un-un! I'm too mad right now. And where the hell are y'all ski masks? Y'all wasn't supposed to show your faces."

"C'mon, Em. We ain't got time for this naggin' shit right now. Show me where you found that paper, so we can be out."

Still pissed at how he'd handled me, I rolled my eyes and shuffled off.

Ten minutes later, Shark had cleared Vladir's entire stash. He'd gotten all the money, jewelry, and everything else of value. I knew it was wrong for me to rob somebody I considered a friend, but I really needed this. Shit at home had gotten so out of hand. This money was going to be a down payment on a new life for me.

"Say, I want you to go out to the car and wait for us. I'm 'bout to go handle this nigga and get Birdie," Shark stated.

"Hol' up. That wasn't part of the plan. All we were supposed to do was rob him. That's it!" I whispered harshly.

"I know what I said, but it's been a change of plans. Dude ran his mouth too much. Plus, I didn't like how he was lookin' at you."

"No, Shark. I'm not gon' let you kill him! That man ain't did nothing to me."

I felt bad enough about robbing Vladir. The last thing I wanted was for him to lose his life.

Shark reached back and smacked the dog shit out of me. "You hardheaded. The one thing I ain't gon' deal with is a bitch that don't listen! Plus, why the fuck it matters if he lives or not? You must be fuckin' this nigga for real."

My eyes widened in shock. *Who is this man? This clearly ain't the same Shark I'd been dealing with. He would never hit me.*

Before I could process everything, several shots rang out. Me and Shark both jumped.

Pow! Pow!

"Fuck was that!" Shark looked around frantically.

"I don't know. Let's just leave."

"Fuck nah. I'm not leaving my nigga!" he belted.

"Come with me. Please! Something don't feel right about this."

I had this feeling in my gut that shit was about to take a turn for the worst.

"Go to the muthufuc—"

Shark's words were abruptly cut short when a bullet pierced the front of his head and exited the back. When his blood splattered on my face, I let out a gut-wrenching scream.

It was a hole in his head almost the size of a golf ball. I glanced over to my left and noticed Vladir clutching his side. Blood was pouring out profusely. I could see that he was seriously hurt by the way his face contorted.

I gave Shark one last look before I finally took off running. It wasn't until I was about six blocks from Vladir's house when I finally stopped. *What the fuck just happened? What am I going to do now?*

Emera

Five years later…

"**H**ey, boo. You got somebody in platinum wanting a private dance." My homegirl, Kitty, approached me.

I'd just left the stage from doing my third set of the evening. After milking the crowd for over two Gs, I was ready to take a small break. Too bad people didn't know how to let me be.

"Damn. Do these niggas ever get tired of seeing ass? My damn feet are on fire. Plus, I'm tired as hell," I complained.

"Persia, what have I always told you?" she asked, referring to me by my stage name. I sucked my teeth.

"The only thing we turn down are our Chucks."

"Exactly. It's been slow as hell in here tonight, and niggas been acting hella cheap. Yet somehow, yo' ass don' managed to get all the bread. You better get yo' big booty over there before I get that paper myself," she fussed while waving a finger in my face.

Kitty was the only dancer that I fucked with at the club. She was a Latina chick that stood about five feet eight with a cinnamon complexion, doe-shaped eyes, honey-blonde hair, bowlegs, and big watermelon breasts. The Spanish and Latin men couldn't get enough of her.

When I first started at Club Bounce, I didn't know shit about being a stripper. Kitty made me her protégé and schooled me on the ins and outs. After almost five years in, and I was now the highest-paid dancer.

"A'ight. I guess you right. His ass better be worth it 'cause my feet are screaming."

She laughed.

"He will definitely be worth it."

"I'll be the judge of that." I turned and made a beeline for the VIP.

***

"Hey. I heard you wanted a dance." I walked up to the dude that was seated in VIP across from the main stage.

To give a quick break down of the club, it consisted of three areas: general seating, first-class seating, and platinum seating. The general seating was pretty much self-explanatory. Only broke muthafuckas that didn't tip, get dances, or buy liquor sat over there.

First-class seating was what we dancers referred to as the fake ballers' section. Usually, dudes that wore cheap jewelry, popped bottles of Moscato, and made it rain with their rent money sat in that area. They'd blow their whole check in one night and cry about it for the rest of the week.

Now the platinum seating was where we'd find the real go-getters. As such, the minimum price for a booth started at $2500. That was pocket change for them. Those niggas came into the club wearing houses on their wrists, Bentleys in their ears, and paychecks on their teeth. They would easily drop no less than ten grand within the first twenty minutes.

"'Sup with ya? How you doin' this evening?" he asked in a raspy voice.

Ol' boy was light brown with a slender nose, bright-hazel eyes, and soft, full lips. Wearing Balmain from head to toe and drinking Cristal, I knew he had that paper. *Kitty hit the mark with this one.*

"Do you know me from somewhere?" I asked.

"Nah. Why you say that?"

"Because only my regulars ask for me." I threw my hands on my hips.

He slightly chuckled. "Be easy, ma. I just saw yo' lil' performance and thought you did a good job. So can you give me a dance or not?"

"It depends. The price for a private dance is $150. There is absolutely no touching, and you can't be doing weird shit like jacking off. You think you can handle that?" I asked with a roll of my neck.

He licked his thick lips as his eyes took in my body. "I think I can handle it," he finally responded with his gaze on my hips.

"Hey, my eyes are up here," I told him, and he smirked.

By now, I was used to men gawking at me. I was five feet six with a mahogany complexion, perky D-cup breasts, baby-bearing hips, and a nice, high booty like Ebony's from the *Player's Club.* Although I preferred to rock sew-ins, my naturally kinky hair was to the middle of my back. I kept it hidden because I hated the lion look.

Five minutes later, we were in the back of the club where we performed our private shows. It wasn't anything fancy about the room. There was only an armless chair, purple shag carpet, and a small radio.

Clad only in a pink thong bikini, I seductively strutted over to him as the old-school song "Wetter" by Twista crooned from the speakers.

> *I'm calling you daddy (daddy)*
> *Can you be my daddy (daddy)*
> *I need a daddy (daddy)*
> *Won't you be my daddy (daddy)*
> *Come and make it rain down on me…*

After sliding down onto his lap, I started with a simple booty-clap dance. This was a way for me to get warmed up before moving on to the main show. It was also a way for me to weed out the perverts. If a guy couldn't make it through a booty dance without grabbing me, he damn sure couldn't handle my nude performance.

To my unpleasant surprise, ol' boy didn't seem pressed. He had this nonchalant look plastered on his face. I couldn't say whether it was boredom or just seriousness. *Okay, he wanna play tough. I'm about to kick this shit up a notch!*

After sliding off his lap, I brought my right leg around and fell into a hard split. My ass cheeks were like thunder as I proceeded to hammer the floor with them. *Smack! Smack! Smack!* They clapped. I glanced back just in time to see a little smirk on his face.

I stood up and rolled the thongs down to my ankles. After stepping one foot out, I used the other to kick my panties at him. He cracked a big ass grin and then motioned with his finger for me to come back.

Doing as I was told, I seductively strutted over and straddled him. With the hardness of his dick poking my inner thigh, I hit his ass with the coup de grâce. I fell into a backbend and flexed my legs open and closed.

Unable to resist, the guy slid his finger down to my clit and gave it a gentle squeeze. Now there were two things I could have done at that moment: either remind him of the no-touching rule or leave. I chose neither. His touch set off a surge of electricity that sent my clit into overdrive. Stunned, I hadn't felt that feeling before. That nigga had the magic touch for real.

Emera, what the hell are you doing? Don't let him mind fuck you like this. My head was screaming one thing, but my body was telling me something different. I felt so conflicted.

"Come home with me," he leaned in and whispered.

At that exact moment, my common sense kicked in, leading me to spring off his lap.

"Hell no! I ain't no hoe, and this pussy ain't for sale."

"Pipe down, ma. I wouldn't have asked you to come home if I thought you did this with everybody."

"I'm sorry, but I never mix business with pleasure." I bent over and picked up my thong.

"So that was all business for you?" he asked, stroking his goatee.

"Nothing more, nothing less." I lied.

"Dig that," he told me with a sly smirk.

I watched as he adjusted himself inside his pants and stood up. He reached into his pocket and pulled out a fat knot. I didn't know why, but my body started to tremble when he approached me.

"Here you go."

I stared at the fat knot in confusion. "The dance was only $150."

"I know. That's just a little something extra for the overtime you put in." With those last words, he dropped the knot in my hand and disappeared.

"Oh my goodness," was all I could say as I unrolled the wad of cash.

Emera

Two days later…

"Unfortunately, the board has declined her offer to join the women's organization. Her past was too sketchy, and those teenage girls are very impressionable," Lola stated.

"C'mon, ma. That's ridiculous. There are plenty of ex-drug addicts that are now model citizens. Why should your past determine your future?" Nolen questioned.

"Because if she used drugs once, there is a big chance she'll do it again. Besides, this could all be a plot to rob us blind. You just can't trust those types of people."

I rolled my eyes and sighed. "Is there a problem, Emera?" Lola asked.

"No, there's no problem." I flashed a fake smile.

I was at a country club having lunch with my boyfriend, Nolen, and his bougie mama. After I ran away from Oklahoma, I came to Fayetteville, a city in Northwest Arkansas. Nobody knew me here, so it was easy for me to start a new life.

Nolen and I had been together for two years, but he didn't know that I was a stripper. He thought that I did bottle service. I lied because I didn't want him to look at me differently.

Nolen's family was very prestigious. His grandfather was a big-time development mogul that owned most of the buildings in the city. They had a company called Aberdeen's Development, where Lola was the president, and Nolen was the CEO.

I liked Nolen a lot. He was kind and gentle, and he provided me with a sense of stableness. The thing was, I wasn't in love with him. Whenever we were together, it felt like I was living a double life. I couldn't be myself, and that bothered me.

"Tell me something. Emera? How long do you plan to work at the club?" Lola queried.

"What does that have to do with this conversation?"

"I'm just wondering. Are you waiting to build up a pension or something?"

"Seriously? We gonna do this right now?" Nolen sighed.

"Oh hush, Nolen. She's a big girl. I'm sure if she can handle those creepy men staring at her daily, then she can handle this simple question."

I sat back in my seat and glared at Lola. How dare her build-a-body, Botoxed face ass try to speak on what I did for a living?

"I don't see what the issue is. I like my job, and I'm not hurting anybody."

"The issue is that you're a bottle waitress at a club. My correction, I mean a strip club. Whereas my son is the CEO of our company. He holds an MBA in business, does charity with various organizations, and plays golf with our mayor. Do you see where I'm going with this? It would be suicidal for him to attend a business meeting with you on his arm. At the very best, you could offer advice on the top brands of champagne. And what about marriage? Do you actually think he'll marry you?"

"I don't know, but it's really not your business if he decides to or not."

"Oh, it most certainly is my business. I have a company to protect. There is no way I will allow Nolen to risk what we've built by marrying you. I'll cut him off before I let that happen," she snarled.

I jumped up and pushed my chair back.

"You know what, Lola? You really need to find a man quick 'cause this overzealous obsession with your son is not healthy. I swear you want to fuck him," I spat, and everyone around us gasped. "And FYI, I don't wanna marry your son. Not until you pop your titty out of his mouth."

Lola's eyes widened in shock as I raced out of the country club. When I finally made it outside, I took my phone out to give Kitty a call. She was the only one that knew how to calm me in situations like this.

"Hey, girl," she answered on the first ring.

"I need a drink. Can you meet me?"

"Oh, Lord. What happened?"

"Lola's bitch ass is what happened. She just belittled the fuck out of me, and Nolen didn't say shit."

"That's not cool, Persia. I don't care if that is his mama. His ass should've stood up for you. No offense, but your man needs to get some bigger balls."

"It is what it is. Can you meet me?"

"Of course, mami. Austin is with his dad, so my evening is free. Where you trying to go?"

I told Kitty to meet me at JJ's Bar and Grill on Wedington. After she agreed, I ended the call. A small part of me had hoped that Nolen would come to check on me. It never happened.

Emera

A few weeks later…

I had just finished a set and was ready to work the room when something happened. Ol' boy entered the building. I was shocked to see him because he hadn't shown his face since that night.

As he made his way through the club, his presence garnered a lot of attention. While all the dancers stood around gawking, the men sat with their mugs on. They were probably pissed that their shine had been stolen.

My heart started beating ten miles per minute as I watched him stroll to the platinum section. Taking his seat of choice, he glanced around as if he was looking for somebody.

"Damn, bitch! Who is that?" I heard one of the dancers, Selis, ask another dancer.

"I'on know. He came in here one other night and got a private dance from Persia. This the first time I don' seen him back."

When I heard my name, I glanced in their direction. Selis cut her eyes at me before whispering something to the other dancer. They both glanced back at me and started snickering. I brushed them off and put my focus back on ol' boy.

To my surprise, he was already looking in my direction. I was ready to step to him when Selis swooped in and sat on his lap. Leaning in, she put her titties against his chest and whispered in his ear. He laughed and whispered something back to her. I felt a pang of jealousy as I watched them out the corner of my eye.

Suddenly, Selis hopped off his lap and stormed off.

"Say, c'mere," I heard him yell over the music.

"You talking to me?"

"Who else would I be talking to?"

As if I was annoyed, I strutted over to him and put my hands on my hips. "Wassup?"

"I'm trying to get a private dance. You available?"

"Uh, I was just about to work the room," my ass said, knowing damn well I didn't care about that. A bitch just didn't want to come off as too pressed.

"How about I pay you double of what I gave you last time? Will that be enough to make you put that on pause?"

Hell yeah. I would have done it for the regular amount. "I mean, I guess I can wait until I finish your dance."

"Bet."

He stood up to follow me to the back. Just before I made it to the private room, Kitty grabbed my hand.

"Hey. Mont wants you," she said.

"Tell him I'll come see him in a minute. I'm about to do a private dance."

"He said he needs to see you ASAP."

"Really? A'ight damn." Kitty walked away as I turned and faced the guy. "Give me a few minutes. I need to handle something right quick."

His eyes roamed my body before settling back on my face. "You know where to find me," he said before strolling off.

This shit better be important, or I'ma curse Mont's ass out.

"Wassup, Mont? Please make this quick. I got somebody waiting on a private dance," I said as I made it to his office.

Mont, the owner of the club, was brown-skinned with a small stature. He kind of put me in the mind of Stevie J from *Love & Hip Hop: Atlanta.*

"Come in and close the door. This will only take a couple of minutes," he told me and then directed me to a seat in front of his desk. I declined his offer.

"I got a proposition for you."

"What's that?"

"Some of the girls have been fighting again."

"Okay... What that got to do with me?"

"I wanna make you the house mother. You're about the only one who doesn't get involved in all that childish bullshit. I feel you will be good at getting and keeping the girls in line."

"I don't know, Mont. All I really want to do is just make my money and go home. I'm not feeling all this extra stuff."

"C'mon, Persia. You 'bout the only one I can count on. Plus, if you do this for me, then I'll let you keep your payout."

I lifted a brow. Keeping my payout would mean more take-home money, which in turn would allow me to move out of Nolen's place and find my own crib.

"A'ight, fuck it! I'll give it a try. If one of those hoes test me, it's a wrap."

"That's my girl. I knew I could count on you."

I walked over to the door. "Hol' up. We need to have a meeting to go over a few things. Get Kitty to do your private dance."

"I can't pass him off to somebody else. He talking about pay—" I suddenly cut myself off. There was no way I could tell Mont's greedy ass that the guy was going to pay me six thousand dollars. He'd probably try to be low down and get a cut.

"What was that?"

"Nothing. I'll just tell him that I'll catch him some other time."

I walked out of the office before Mont could say something else. When I made it back to the floor, I glanced around and noticed the dude sitting in his seat. I strutted over to him.

"Hey, so about that dance…"

"It's cool, ma. We can do it some other time," he said, finishing my sentence.

I watched as he tossed a fifty on the table and stood up. He was so tall that I had to look up at him.

"This is why we need to go back to my crib. It won't be no interruptions there."

I pressed my lips together and shook my head.

"Next time, I ain't gon' let you get off that easy. The only reason I'm letting you slide now is because I had business to handle anyway." He smacked me on the booty and winked his eye at me.

"Make sure you keep that thang wet for me," he said, and I blushed.

Emera

One month later…

I was leaving the grocery store when I passed a lady that looked familiar. She must have noticed me too because she turned back around and just stared at me.

"Emera, is that you?" she finally asked.

"Ms. London?" I questioned with a surprised look.

"Mhm," she said, and a big smile covered her face.

"What are you doing here?"

Ms. London was one of my mom's closest friends when I was growing up. They used to get high together. I guess that was why I didn't recognize her. The last time I saw Ms. London, she was looking like a real fiend. Most of her teeth were rotten, her eyes were sunken in, and she was about the size of my pinky. She looked like a completely different person with her two-piece suit on, roller-set hair, and new shiny teeth.

"I'm here at a church convention. My pastor will be

preaching at St. John tomorrow."

"Wow! You look good, Ms. London."

"So do you, honey. You've really grown into a beautiful young lady. Is this where you've been all this time?"

"Yes, ma'am."

"Girl, we were all worried about you when you ran away. To be honest, we thought you were dead. Your mama stressed herself out, looking all over for you. She started hitting that pipe even harder than before. Why would you put her through that?"

Hearing the mention of my mama sent a pain to my chest. I would be lying if I said I didn't wonder how she was doing.

"My life was horrible there. Mama had all those men coming in and out. On top of that, she was beating me for no reason."

"I know, chile. To be honest, I can't blame you. With all the stuff that me and your mama had going on, it's no wonder we ain't dead. Those drugs were something serious. Hell, it took me hitting rock bottom three times before I finally decided to get my life on track. I'm three years clean in two weeks."

"That's so good to hear," I said, and she slightly smiled at me.

"She still hasn't kicked that habit, Emera. I know she wants to, but it just ain't happened yet," she said, seemingly reading my mind.

"I don't think so. If she hasn't done it in all this time, it's not gon' happen. But it was good seeing you, Ms. London. Good luck on your journey." I turned to walk away before the tears I was holding fell down my cheeks.

"Wait, Emera. Can I at least give you her number? You don't have to reach out right now. Just whenever the Lord puts it on your heart to do so."

"No. I'd rather not go there. And please don't tell her that you saw me."

***

"Do you have to go in tonight? I wanted to spend some time together," Nolen asked as I applied a layer of red lipstick.

"Yup. I gotta be there to keep the other girls in line. I told you that."

"Damn it, Emera. I've been trying to spend time with you, but you keep blowing me off for that stupid club. We haven't been having sex, and you barely look at me. What's the problem?"

My neck snapped around like the little girl on the *Exorcist*.

"Oh, so now we got some balls?"

"What is that supposed to mean?" Nolen walked over and stood in front of me.

Nolen was the average height for a man with an athletic build, yellow complexion, and wavy hair. I had never seen his dad, but I imagined that was who he resembled. From what Nolen's cousin Aubrey told me, Nolen's father was a white man. He and Lola dated a few years before her father put an end to it. He was on some old-school mess, not wanting Lola to date outside her race. He told Lola that if she didn't stop seeing dude, she wouldn't inherit his company. Apparently, the breakup was what caused Lola to become so bitter.

"What it means is that I'm surprised you got a voice. When your mama is around, you seem to tuck your tail between your legs."

"Are you still mad about what she said?"

"No. I'm used to her behavior. I'm angry because you didn't stand up for me. You've never stood up for me, Nolen."

Nolen dropped to his knees in front of me.

"I'm sorry, Emera. How can I make it up to you? I don't like it when we fight."

"Grow some damn balls and be a man. That's what you can do."

I looked myself over one last time in the mirror before grabbing my purse. Nolen grabbed my arm as I was leaving.

"I really love you, Emera. No matter what my mother says, I'm going to make you my wife."

"The sad part is that you really believe the bullshit you're spitting."

***

Hours later...

All night, I had been on pins and needles waiting for the mystery man to show up. He never came. After a while, I finally stopped watching the door and focused on my money. The club was full of high rollers.

In just the first two hours, I made over three thousand dollars. Several men tried to get private dances, but I couldn't do it. For some reason, I felt like I would be betraying him. Silly, right?

"Hey, what's the problem?" I walked into the dressing room just as Kitty and Selis were about to come to blows.

"This bitch keeps trying to take my customers. I don' told her hoe ass to stay away from what's mine. Maybe if you clean that pussy, you can get your own customers. Fuckin' puta!" Kitty yelled while pointing her finger in Selis's face.

"You better get that finger out my face," Selis barked back.

"What you gon' do if I don't?"

Selis pushed Kitty into one of the booths, causing her head to slam against the mirror.

"Ah, hell nah! I'm about to kill this bitch!" Kitty barked.

"Hol' up!" I said, grabbing hold of Selis, who was trying her best to swing at Kitty.

Their commotion drew in some of the dancers and one of the bouncers.

"Is there a problem?" the bouncer, Chris, asked.

"Can you please escort Selis out for me? Selis, you are suspended for two days."

"What! You can't suspend me." She jumped into my face.

"First of all, back the hell up. Secondly, I can suspend you for fighting."

Selis glowered at me. "This is so fucked up! We gon' see what Mont says when he finds out you fucked with his money."

"Hoe, you ain't making no money. All that dick you be sucking in the back, and your pockets are still dry," Kitty spat. The room erupted with laughter.

"Yo, chill, Kitty. I'm trying to handle this."

"Okay, mami. I'm just so angry."

"This shit ain't over, bitch!" Selis yelled as the bouncer dragged her out.

"Thanks for having my back," Kitty told me.

"C'mon now. You know you're my girl. Plus, I can't stand that bitch. She needs to go see a doctor with that funky pussy," I said, and Kitty started giggling.

"You ready to leave? I need to go home and check on my baby."

"Just give me a minute to grab my things."

Ten minutes later, me and Kitty were heading outside.

"See you later. Make sure you text me once you make it home," I told her.

"I gotcha."

I went to my car and unlocked the trunk.

"Waddup, ma," I heard somebody say, and I jumped.

"Ah, shit! You scared the hell out of me."

"My bad about that," he said with a slight chuckle.

"What you doin' here?" I breathed heavily.
A big part of me was happy to see him, although I wish he would have shown up earlier.

"I came to get my dance."

"You a little too late. I'm 'bout to head out."

"Look, ma. Let's cut the bullshit. It's obvious we feelin' each other, so you might as well have dinner with a nigga."

"Wow! That was the best dinner proposal I ever got," I stated sarcastically.

"What you wanted me to say? 'Will you please have dinner with me,' like those corny muthafuckas? Nah, that ain't me. I asked you out. You may not like how I did it, but that's who I am. Either you can choose to accept it or not."

I shook my head and let out a small giggle. "Yo' hood ass is crazy. I don't even know your name."

"It's Rocco. What's yours? And don't give me your stripper name either."

"It's Emera."

"Dig that. Now can I please have your number so I can take you out?" he asked in a proper voice. I busted out laughing.

"Boy, give me your damn phone," I spat playfully.

"On the real, ma, I'ma show you a good time." He handed me his phone.

"We'll see."

Emera

Rocking a fitted, black Tory Burch dress and six-inch, peep-toed Giuseppe Zanotti heels, I strutted up to the door of Ruth's Chris Steakhouse. Although I was feeling a little nervous, you would never be able to tell as my walk exuded confidence.

"Mhm," I said, clearing my throat as I approached him.

When Rocco glanced up and saw me standing there, a big smile covered his face. "Damn, ma. You look good as fuck."

"Thanks. You don't look so bad yourself."

Rocco was draped in Versace all the way down to his feet. His low fade was freshly cut, and the diamond-studded earrings in his ears were blinging.

"You ready to get this date started?"

"Yes."

Rocco held the door for me to step inside. After confirming our reservation with the hostess, she took us to a table located toward the restaurant's back. Rocco was a gentleman by pulling out my chair.

"Look at you trying to earn some brownie points."

He flashed me a sexy grin. "Whatcha mean? I'm a gentleman."

When the waitress came to take our orders, Rocco and I both decided on the surf and turf combo with a bottle of Merlot wine.

"How old are you?" I asked.

"Twenty-two. How old are you?"

"The same age as you."

"That's wassup. What you like doing for fun?"

"Don't laugh, okay?" I told him.

"What? You like playing with dolls or som' shit like that?"

"No. I actually like to skate, but I haven't done it since I was a teenager. And I like playing card games, like UNO."

Rocco laughed.

"I told you not to laugh." Reaching across the table, I smacked his arm.

"It's cool, ma. I'm just tripping because you a lot different from what I thought." He sat back in his seat and gazed at me.

"Different how?"

"You got this innocence about you that don't show when you at the club. It's almost like you're hiding behind someone else when you dancin'."

"Men come into the club, looking to get their fantasies fulfilled. If I wanna get my money, then I gotta play the part."

"Do you like stripping?

"I mean, it's a job. I don't love it, but I don't hate it either. If it was something else I could do, I would. Unfortunately, ain't too many people looking to hire a high school dropout. So I gotta take what I can get until something better comes around."

"I fucks with that. On another note, Ms. Persia, can I get a discount on a dance?" he said, and I laughed.

***

A few hours later...

"You know we ain't gotta do this if you don't want to."

"It's okay. I wanna do it," I whispered.

After leaving the restaurant, I agreed to come back to Rocco's house for a spell. My intentions hadn't been to sleep with him, but one thing just sort of led to another. Before I knew it, I was laying on his bed butt ass naked.

Rocco gently massaged my breasts with his big hand and then greedily took one into his mouth. With the precision of a sex expert, he sensually licked all around it before dipping over to the other. Squeezing them together with his hands, he rotated back and forth between each breast.

"Mmm." A soft moan escaped my lips.

If this man's tongue game was this vicious, I could only imagine what the dick was like.

Once he'd made my nipples hard as bricks, Rocco trailed his tongue to my stomach. He placed soft kisses around my navel. Taking the kisses further, he stopped right at the area above my triangle.

By now, I had the sheet gripped tightly in my hand from the anticipation of what was to come. The closer he got to my lips, the harder my clit thumped. It was almost as if it had a pulse. He twirled his tongue around a few times and then buried his head in my folds.

My back arched, and my mouth flew wide open. With the softness of his lips combined with the swiftness of his tongue, he'd brought me to a peak in under one minute.

"Oh, shit! I'm cumming!" I yelled, and my body jerked forth. I'd never come so hard and so fast in all my life. It was actually a little embarrassing.

Rocco didn't even give me the chance to recover before he slithered between my legs and plunged deep inside. With only one mission, he went straight to my G-spot and zoned in on it. Delivering stroke after stroke, he commenced to leaving a mark that only he could recover. He lowered his head and drew a nipple into his mouth. Biting down gently, he introduced me to the world of pain mixed with pleasure.

I took my nails and dug them into his back. The harder he stroked, the harder I dug. He wrapped his hand around my neck and applied a little pressure. I felt a tingling sensation in my legs, indicating another orgasm was about to come.

"Fuck!" Rocco groaned while biting his bottom lip.

He put a sensual kiss on my shoulder before pulling out. Flipping me on all fours, he grabbed a fist full of hair. I gasped when he thrust into me from the back.

"Ugh," I let out as he pushed himself deeper.

He was so deep that I could now feel him in my stomach. I put my hand on his waist to stop him from going further, but he pushed it off.

"Nah. I want you to feel every inch of this hard dick. Matter of fact, fuck me back," he demanded.

I threw my ass against him, and he smacked it. *Tap!*

"Keep going. I want to feel that pussy get soaking wet."

I did it again and again until I felt my legs shake.

"Ah, fuck! I'm 'bout to nut!" Rocco grunted.

By now, my body was so spent that I could barely stay upright. Rocco had to cradle me in his arms to keep me from falling over. It was at that moment when I realized that I'd fucked up. *What the hell have I done?*

Emera

Three weeks later…

"**S**top, Rocco." I giggled hysterically as he picked me up and tossed me on the bed.

I'd tried my best to stay away from Rocco after the first time we had sex. Any time he would call, I would send him to voicemail. Whenever he sent text messages, I left them unread. That lasted for all of two days before I finally gave in.

Unable to avoid the inevitable, I came running right back to him. That was over two weeks ago, and I hadn't been able to stay away.

"You gon' learn to quit playing with me, shawty. What I tell ya about giving private dances to other niggas, huh?' He put his hands on the sides of my head and stared down at me.

My eyes went to those soft, sexy lips, and my panties got wet. *Why am I so infatuated with this man?*

"What was I supposed to do? Mont would've flipped if I didn't do that dance."

"Man, you need to just quit that place. You can find something else to do."

"Trust me, I wanna get away from the club more than you

know it. It's just that I can't leave right now. I need to get my money up first."

"Why you in such a rush to move? Ol' girl giving you a hard time?"

"Some like that."

"If shit is that bad, you can just come stay with me."

"Rocco, seriously? We've only known each other for what... like an hour. I can't just move in with you. That's silly."

"You can be with somebody for years and still not know them. Time don't mean shit."

I gazed into his eyes. *Why was he playing with my head like this?* Didn't he know that I was ready to risk it all at any minute? Him giving me another reason wasn't helping.

"Can you get up? I gotta leave so I can get to work."

This was all starting to be too much. I needed to get away from him before allowing my emotions to write a check that my reality couldn't cash.

"What if I wanted you to stay with me tonight?"

"I can't. Tonight is our annual battle of the strippers. I could miss out on a lot of money."

"How much do you generally make on a night like that?"

"I don't know. Like three thousand dollars. Why?"

Rocco slid off the bed and strolled to his dresser. After digging inside the drawer, he came back and dropped a roll of bills on my lap.

"I'll pay you sixty-five hundred for one dance—right here. So what's up."

This shit is crazy! "Um..." I hesitated.

"It's simple, ma. Go dance for a bunch of niggas for half the price, or do one dance for me."

"Rocco, your ass is crazy. But I guess, when you put it like that, it makes the deal hard to resist."

Rocco climbed on top of me and put his head against mine.

"You know I'm not gon' really make you dance." He leaned in and covered my lips with his.

Emera

A few weeks later...

"Yo, that was crazy. Did you see all that money they were throwing at us? I can't wait to count these earnings," Kitty said with a big grin as we headed to the dressing room.

Every Wednesday, we had this showcase where all the girls would team up and put on a joint performance. It was something that Mont had come up with to bring in extra money. He knew that everybody loved a little girl-on-girl action. Me and Kitty didn't actually do sexual activities, but we sold the hell out of the allusion.

"Hey, is everything okay? You been quiet as hell tonight."

I turned to Kitty with a straight face. "I think I'm in love."

"Okay. You're just now realizing that after several years?"

"No. I'm not talking about with Nolen."

"Who are you talkin' about?"

"This is just between you and me, right?" I asked and

glanced around.

"Yeah." Kitty looked confused.

"I think I'm in love with that guy from the club."

Kitty looked as if she was thinking about it. "Oh shit. You talkin' about the fine one that only gets dances from you?"

"Mhm." I nodded.

Kitty busted out laughing. "Damn, girl. I didn't think you could fall in love off just a lap dance."

When I didn't say anything, her eyes got wide as saucers.

"Wait a minute. Don't tell me that it's been more than a dance."

I bit down on my bottom lip.

"Persia, did you fuck that man?"

"Yes, but I didn't mean to."

She started going crazy. "Bitch! How do you accidentally fuck somebody?"

"Shhh. Keep it down before one of these other hoes hears you. I don't need them all in my business."

"My bad, girl. Was it good?" she squealed.

"So good that I'm thinking about leaving Nolen."

"Hol' up, baby girl, pump your breaks. I hope you're not confusing good sex with love. Trust me, it may feel the same, but it's completely different. I made this same mistake when I messed off on my baby daddy. Two months after fucking the other nigga, and I was ready to go back. I realized very quickly that I'd made a big mistake."

"I get what you're saying. However, this is different. This

feeling that I have for Rocco, I've never had it with Nolen. He gives me butterflies whenever I'm with him. And if we're not together, I can't focus on anything else but getting back to him. Every time I close my eyes, all I see is his face. Hell, I've even considered leaving the club."

"Well, damn. Maybe I am wrong 'cause those are the same feelings I have for my baby daddy. When I messed around with that other guy, all I had were sexual thoughts."

"I'm telling you, Kitty. This man has my head gone."

"Wow! So what are you going to do?" she asked.

"I'on know. I really want to be with Rocco. At the same time, I don't want to hurt Nolen. He's been there for me since day one."

"The heart wants what the heart wants, mami. No matter how hard you try to fight it, love prevails every time."

"Persia, Mont wanna see you," Selis walked in and said.

Surprisingly, she'd been alright since the time I suspended her.

"What he want with me?"

"I'on know. He didn't tell me." She shrugged.

"Go ahead, boo. We can finish this conversation once you get back," Kitty told me.

I sucked my teeth and walked back out to the front. Mont wasn't in the central area, so I went to his office. The lights were on, but he wasn't in there either. *Why he got me looking for him, and he's nowhere to be found?*

"Hey, have you seen Mont?" I asked one of the dancers walking by.

"He left about an hour ago."

"What?" I frowned.

"Yeah, he said he had something to do. He should be back in a couple of hours."

I quickly spun on my heels and ran back to the dressing room. As soon as I made it to the door, I could sense something was wrong. A few of the dancers were standing around crying. I pushed past them and stumbled into the room.

"Kittyyyy!" I let out a loud, blood-curdling scream. "What happened to her?"

Kitty's eyes were closed, and blood was leaking from her mouth and stomach.

"What the fuck happened?" I turned to the group of women and yelled at them.

"I think Selis stabbed her. When I came in, she was running out," this dancer by the name of Hennessy explained. "Is she dead?"

I ignored Hennessy as I dropped to my knees beside Kitty. Gently lifting her head into my arms, I rubbed her forehead. There was so much blood coming out of her stomach that I didn't know what to do.

"Call for help! Why y'all stupid bitches just standing there? Do something!" I began to sob as I tried desperately to get Kitty up. "Oh, Goddddd! Why?"

***

"Yo, shawty," Rocco said, racing to me.

I'd called him on my way to the hospital and had him meet me here.

"I'm so glad to see you." I threw my arms around his neck and buried my head in his chest.

"What's going on? Did you get hurt?" He pulled away and examined my body with his eyes.

"No. It was my friend. One of the other strippers attacked her."

"Damn. Is she gon' be okay?"

"I don't know. She was stabbed in the stomach. Rocco, it was so much blood. I can still
smell it on my hands, even though I washed them a dozen times. Why can I still smell it?"

"A'ight, calm down, ma. I'm sure everything gon' be straight." Rocco pulled me into his arms and rocked me.

"Family of Iesha Lewis," I heard someone say. I glanced up just as an older, white doctor came strolling out.

"I'm her family." I lied.

"What's your name and your relationship to Ms. Lewis?" the doctor questioned.

"My name is Emera Dehorn. Kitt—I mean, Iesha is my cousin. I was with her before the incident occurred."

"I see. Well, I hate to inform you that Ms. Lewis didn't make it."

"Noooo!" I screamed. "What happened? She was still alive when she arrived here. How could she be dead now?"

"Unfortunately, we couldn't stop the bleeding. As you may or may not know, her spleen was punctured. Now, that's all the info I can give you right now. Once the autopsy is concluded, there will be a full report. I'm really sorry for your loss." The doctor patted my shoulder before walking away.

"This is all my fault. I should've known that it was a set up."

"Ain't no way you could've known what was gon' go down. This ain't on you, ma."

I continued to cry into Rocco's chest as he held me.

"Emera," I heard a familiar voice say.

That time when I glanced back, I saw that it was Nolen. I quickly stepped back from Rocco to create some distance.

Nolen's eyes darted to Rocco before focusing on me.

"Uh, Nolen, what are you doing here?"

"I saw a report on the news that someone from your job was stabbed. I thought it was you since you weren't answering your phone. So, I went to the club, and one of the girls told me that you were here. What's going on?" The entire time Nolen spoke, he kept his eyes on Rocco.

"Kitty was killed tonight," I spat.

It didn't even sound right to hear myself speak those words. I glanced at Rocco and noticed him staring upside my head.

"Um, Rocco, this is Nolen."

"Her boyfriend." Nolen finished the introduction.

"Oh yeah? What's going on, homie?" Rocco grumbled while shooting daggers at me.

I used my eyes to apologize for not telling him. The ice-cold glare that he gave me said he didn't accept it.

"I'ma head out. Sorry for your loss again."

When Rocco walked off, I felt a sharp pain in my chest. I didn't know if I would see him again after this.

"Who was that?" Nolen wasted no time asking.

"Just a friend."

"A friend? Why haven't I ever met him before?"

"Damn, Nolen. I just lost my friend, and this is what you on? I don't have time for this." I was ready to walk away when Nolen grabbed my arm.

"Hol' up, Em. That's my bad. I shouldn't have asked you that." He pulled me into his arms and hugged me. "I'm sorry about Kitty. I know how close y'all were."

At that moment, I felt like shit. Not only had I lost Kitty but possibly Rocco all in the same night. On top of that, I was cheating on Nolen. If I didn't hate my life before, I definitely hated it now.

***

I was in a deep sleep when I heard loud shouting in the near distance. Glancing over to my right, I noticed Nolen was no longer laying next to me. I quickly jumped up and followed the voices.

"Nolen, this is crazy! Strippers and stabbings? How do you think that makes us look to the community? We are a prominent family, and that tramp is messing up *our* reputation. I bet your grandfather is rolling over in his grave right now. Why don't you get some damn balls and cut her off!"

"I can't do that, ma."

"Why not?"

"Because I love her. Emera is not a bad person. You would know that if you actually gave her a chance."

"For Christ's sake! You are even more pussy whipped than I thought. What is she doing to you? Sucking your dick with a Halls? She is not who you think she is."

"Why would you say that?"

"I didn't want to mention this before because I knew that you wouldn't believe me."

"Believe you about what?" Nolen asked with a confused look.

"I hired a private detective to follow her. She's been lying all this time. Her ass ain't no damn bottle service person. She's a damn stripper. Not only that, but she's cheating on you."

I finally stepped around the corner, and Lola's eyes got wide.

"Well, I guess you found a way to get me away from your son," I uttered.

"So, this is true?" Nolen asked as I faced him.

"I'm sorry, Nolen." That was the only thing I could think to say. Lola had already put me on blast, so what else could I do?

"There goes your truth, straight from the horse's mouth."

"Get out, Ma!" Nolen shouted.

"Excuse you?"

"You heard me. I said, get out now. Nobody asked you to stick your nose in my business."

"Fine, I'll leave. Let me just say this first. I'm your mother, and I love you. The only reason I interfered is because you were too blind to see past her lies. I couldn't stand by and watch her hurt you."

After grabbing her purse, Lola shot me a mean ass look before she left.

"It's that guy from the hospital, right?"

"Nol—"

"Is it?" he yelled, and I jumped. I had never seen him this angry.

"Mhm," I mumbled as a single tear fell down my cheek. "I'm sorry, Nolen."

"Save your apologies. I knew something was going on when I saw y'all together. Do you love him?" he asked, and my heart dropped.

"Please don't make me say it."

"It's simple. Either you do, or you don't?"

When I didn't say anything, Nolen dropped his head. I was shocked to see tears in his eyes when he finally looked at me again.

"Go get your shit and get out of my house. It was one thing for you to lie about what you did at the club, but cheating on me is where I draw the line."

There was nothing left for me to say, so I did what I was told. After gathering all my things, I left the only stable home I'd ever had.

Emera

Four days later…

I strutted into Club Bounce with only one mission—grab my shit and roll. My days of working here were officially over.

"Hey… hey. You just gon' walk in here past me like you ain't been missing the past few days," Mont barked.

"I lost my friend, Mont. Am I not allowed time off to grieve?"

"Give me just a minute, baby," Mont told the girl he was talking to.

She nodded before switching off to the other end of the bar.

"Persia, I know you going through some things, but we need you down here. Shit has been a real mess. The girls are snappy with the customers, and they crying all over the place. We losing money left and right."

I gave him an incredulous look. "You don't even care that Kitty is dead, do you?"

"C'mon, you know how much I cared about Kitty."

"If that's the case, why are you already hiring someone to

replace her?" I nodded my head in ol' girl's direction.

"I should've known I couldn't get nothing past you. Look, I cared about Kitty, and I hate what happened, but we gotta bring people in that are willing to work. It's just business. Nothing personal."

"Fuck you, Mont! I'm done with you and this stupid ass club."

I walked away, and Mont grabbed my arm.

"Hol' up, Persia. You can't quit. I really need you. What can I do to make you stay?"

"I'm done. It ain't safe here, and you don't give a fuck about none of us. One of our sisters died, and we can't have time to grieve. Have you reached out to Kitty's family to offer your condolences?"

"Huh... I mean, I was gon' get around—" He scratched the back of his head.

"Just what I thought. She has a son that's now motherless, but I bet you haven't offered him a dime."

"Look, I'ma get around to all that."

"Whatever, Mont! All you care about is your money."

"Where you gon' go? To one of those stuffy gentleman clubs up the block? Them white boys ain't gon' treat you like I do."

"The strip club might be your life, but it's not mine. I actually have goals outside of this bullshit." I walked off, and Mont was still talking.

"You'll be back. Just like all the girls that tried to quit on me."

***

When Rocco opened up the door, wearing only his pajama pants, I bit down on my bottom lip. This man exuded sex appeal.

"'Sup?" he asked casually.

"Can I come in for a minute? I need to talk to you."

"Nah. I'm busy right now."

I figured he would react this way. "C'mon, Rocco. I just need to talk to you for a minute."

He stuck his head out the door. "How you get here?"

"I took an Uber," I said, and he smirked.

After finally stepping back, he held the door for me to enter.

I walked into his place and noticed he'd decorated a little. Before, there wasn't any furniture in the living room. Now, there was a sofa and loveseat, a glass coffee table, and an entertainment center with a big seventy-inch TV.

"I miss you," I told him, and he let out a hearty chuckle.

"Yo, you gotta be kidding right now. How the fuck you gon' miss me with a whole nigga at the crib?"

"I know you're mad at me right now—"

"Why would I be mad? That shit with us wasn't serious. All we were doing was fuckin', right?"

I blinked rapidly to fight back my tears.

"Maybe that's all it meant to you, but to me, it was a lot more. I actually caught feelings for you."

"Whatever, man. You'll stand here and tell me anything

just for a nigga to break you off some dick. Then once I'm finished fuckin' yo' brains out, you'll run home to play house with ol' boy. I know what it is."

I went over to Rocco and tried to wrap my arms around his waist. "Yo, on the real, I'ma need you to bounce."

I folded my arms across my breasts.

"No. I'm not leaving until you hear me out. I, at least, deserve the opportunity to explain."

Once again, Rocco laughed in my face. "Fuck outta here with that. I ain't gotta listen to shit you say."

"I don't care about you being mad. I'm not going anywhere."

"So you ain't gon' leave my shit?" he spat.

"Nope."

I was dead set on standing my ground. That is until Rocco picked me up and threw me over his shoulder. As if he was holding a bag of trash, he carried my ass straight for the door.

"Put me down! Put me down!" I was pounding on his back while kicking my legs.

All of a sudden, he drove my body into the wall. My feet were dangling as my body was suspended in the air.

"You think I'm playing with you! I will fuckin' body yo' ass in here. Quit fuckin' testing me!" he barked before dropping me.

Any sane person would've been scared by this outburst, but not me. I was so turned on that my pussy was dripping. I grabbed Rocco's head and put a kiss on his lips. He pushed me back into the wall and glared at me. I half expected for him to lay me out at that moment. Instead, he yanked down his pants with one hand and spun me around with the other. After lifting my dress over my ass, he slid my panties to the side.

"Is this what you wanted, huh?" he asked, ramming inside of me.

My body slammed against the wall as he delivered fast and angry strokes.

"Oh, yes! Fuck this pussy!" I yelled while placing my palms on the wall.

Rocco pulled halfway out and then slammed back into me. My legs shook violently, and I squirted.

"Ah shit… I'm cumming."

After spreading my butt cheeks, he started to hammer my middle. I couldn't lie; my kitty was literally throbbing from the pounding. Even so, I was enjoying every minute of this dicking down.

"Arghhhhhhh." He suddenly gritted.

When Rocco pulled out, all I could do was slide to the floor. We were quiet for a minute before he finally broke the silence.

"A'ight, so you got what you wanted. Now get the fuck out of my shit!"

No this motherfucker didn't!

<h1 style="text-align:center">Emera</h1>

Three weeks later...

"Although I think you have a great personality, I just don't feel this position is the best fit for you," the manager said, and my smile dropped.

"May I ask why you feel that way?"

"Well, we're looking for a more polished candidate."

No this bastard didn't! I'll show yo' ass unpolished! "I understand. Thank you for your consideration."

I stood up and shook the guy's hand. Even though I was beyond pissed, I couldn't give him the satisfaction of seeing me come undone. That would have proved his point.

"Hey, Emera."

"Yes," I responded as politely as I could.

"Don't take this the wrong way, but if you're free tonight, I'd love to take you out."

Wow! This asshole had a lot of nerve. How dare he tell me

that I wasn't good enough to work for him, yet he wanted to take me on a date?

"Actually, I'm dating someone. Thanks for the offer."

"That's too bad," he said with his eyes roaming my body.

With a disgusted look, I turned and stomped out of the office. When I finally made it to the outside door, I broke down crying.

In the past week, I'd been on five interviews—five. Essentially, all the managers had provided the same feedback. Either I was underqualified or not the right fit for the company. I just didn't get it. Was I that rough around the edges?

The more I thought about the situation, the angrier I became. *Why should I care about saving face when I was just violated?* Storming back into the building, I made a beeline right down the hall to the manager's office. I was ready to go inside when something halted me.

"Yeah, she just left."

"Good. How did it go?"

"I told her that I was looking for somebody more polished."

"Really. How did she react? I would have loved to been a fly on that wall."

"I can tell she didn't take it well. But to be honest, I think she would have been a good fit. She seemed like a nice person. Besides, I would have loved to see that lil' fine thing prancing around here daily."

"Jacob, please! I swear you men are so shallow. All you care about are big asses."

"Do I sense jealousy, Lola?" Jacob laughed.

"None at all. I know that I'm much prettier than she is, and I have class."

Nah, bitch. You're pathetic is what you are!

"If you say so. Anyway, what's the deal with you and her?"

"That's the hoe I told you about that was dating Nolen. I don't want that bitch with my son."

"That's crazy, Lola. Nolen is a grown man. You can't pick and choose who he deals with."

"I'll be damned. Anyway, let me call you back. I have a client that just came in." Lola rushed him off the line.

That was my cue to make my presence known. Pushing the door open, I entered the office. Judging by the look on Jacob's face, he knew he was busted.

"Um, did you forget something?" He fumbled with a few papers that he tried to pick up.

"I guess I should be flattered that you actually saw me as a good candidate."

"Listen…"

"Mmm-mmm. No need for explanations. Just know that your time at this company is about to end."

With my head held high, I turned and walked back out the door.

***

"You can stop right here. I shouldn't be too long," I told the Uber driver.

After stepping out of the car, I marched right up to the door of Aberdeen's Development."

"Hi, ma'am. Do you have an appointment?" the front receptionist asked.

I strutted right past like I didn't hear her.

"Ma'am, do you have an appointment? Ma'am!"

Nolen's office door was closed when I got to it, so I pushed it open.

"Emera, what are you doing here?"

I shot my eyes at the woman standing in front of him. Recognition immediately hit me as to who she was. It was Nolen's ex, Olivia. She was a tall, chocolate, super-model chick who he dated before we met. *I see it didn't take this nigga long to move on.*

"Tell your mama to stay the fuck out of my business! If she keeps harassing me, then I'll have her tight faced ass locked up."

"What are you talking about?"

"Oh, God. This is so ghetto," Olivia mumbled while rolling her eyes.

"Bitch, I ain't talking to you! Mind yo damn business!"

Olivia shook her head. "I'm going to get your mother so she can handle this. Stand up to her, Nolen."

When Olivia walked past me with a stank look, I fought the urge to slap the shit out of her.

"Emera, this is crazy. Why are you barging in here threatening my mother and calling her names?"

"I just left my fifth interview this week, and you wanna know why?"

"Why?"

"Apparently, your mama told the interviewers not to hire me."

"That's silly, Em. How would she know about your interviews?"

"I'm not sure, but she knows. I just left my last interview at Tyson, and I overheard her talking to the manager."

"I've already called security, so you better leave if you don't want to get thrown out." Lola marched into Nolen's office like a madwoman. Olivia was right on her heels.

"Ma, did you have something to do with Emera interviews?"

"What? That's bizarre! This girl has lost her mind. She can't blame me because no one wants to hire an ex-stripper."

"How did you know that I wasn't working at the club anymore? You still got somebody following me, don't you?" I folded my arms across my breasts and glared at her.

"Huh? What? It's pretty obvious if you're out looking for a job," she stammered.

"Ma, just tell the truth. You did this, didn't you?"

"Nolen, that's your mother. Don't be disrespectful."

"Leave, Olivia. This doesn't have anything to do with you."

"That's probably best because you're making me angry."

That time when Olivia walked by, I stuck out my foot. She almost broke her neck trying to brace herself.

"My bad."

"You did that on purpose. Lola was so right about you!"

I smirked as she shuffled out angrily.

"You see, Nolen? She's very sneaky and manipulative," Lola uttered.

"So are you. I know that Emera isn't lying."

"And how do you know that?"

"Because her interview was at Tyson, where your close friend, Jacob, works. Just stop lying. I don't know how you knew about those interviews, but you were wrong to do that!" Nolen sputtered.

"Okay, fine. I did it. I was just trying to protect you."

"Protect me from what?"

"I figured if she left town, y'all wouldn't be able to reconcile. And then you could marry Olivia, the woman you were meant to be with."

I faced Nolen with my finger pointed at him. "I blame your ass. You should've shut this down from the start, but you didn't. If you wanna know why I cheated on you, well, there's the reason. I'm done with this."

"Emera, wait up. Let me talk to you."

I held up my hand. "You and your crazy ass mama need to stay the hell away from me!"

Emera

It had been a few hours since I left Nolen's office, and he'd been blowing me up ever since. As far as I was concerned, that chapter of my life was now over. Lola's bullshit had made it impossible for me and Nolen to even remain friends. If someone would go to those lengths to keep me away from their son, they had to be bat shit crazy.

My phone rang, bringing me out of my thoughts. When I looked at the caller ID, my eyes lit up. It was Rocco calling. *Should I answer? What the hell am I thinking? Hell yeah, I should answer.*

"Hello." I finally picked up on the fifth ring.

"You left your earrings at my crib."

Really! He gon' use this excuse to call me?

"You can toss them out if you want to."

"Nah, I ain't gon' do that. Just come scoop 'em when you get a chance."

"It's fine. They ain't even real," I responded exasperatedly. Amongst all the other shit I was dealing with, I didn't have time for Rocco's antics.

The line became quiet, but I could still hear Rocco breathing. "Is there anything else you wanted?"

"What's wrong with you? It sounds like you been crying."

"Everything is good." My voice cracked, giving me away.

"You cappin'. Where you at?"

"Rocco."

"Where you at?"

"I'm at the University Hotel off Dickson."

"What you doing there?" he asked.

"It's my home for the time being."

"Come downstairs in like ten minutes. I'm finna pull up."

"Rocco," I called again, but he'd already ended the call.

***

Two hours later…

Me and Rocco were sitting in his room eating sub sandwiches. We hadn't said much since he picked me up an hour ago. To be honest, I didn't know why I was here. The last time, he'd treated me like shit. Even if I deserved it, he didn't have to carry me in that manner. My feelings were seriously hurt.

"What?" I asked when I felt Rocco's eyes on me.

"Why you ain't eating?"
"'Cause I'm not really hungry."

"What happened to you today?"

Rocco took my plate and put it on the nightstand while I explained the situation with Lola.
"Yo, that's some straight bull. What you plan on doing?"

"I'on know. I ain't trying to go back to the club, but that looks like my only option."

"Speaking of the club, why you ain't tell me you quit?"

"I tried to tell you before you put me out."

Rocco chuckled, and I pushed his arm.

"It's not funny."

He got serious and looked into my eyes. "My bad 'bout that. I was still pissed seeing you with ol' boy."

"Rocco…"

"Nah, let me finish," he said, and I nodded. "Look, ma, I ain't in the business of being a side nigga. That shit ain't for me. I'd rather let you go until you decide what you wanna do."

"That's just it, I'm not even with him anymore!" I shouted. "Why do you think I'm living out of a hotel? If you would've just listened to me last time, then I could've explained all of this," I said, and he smirked.

"So y'all don' for real? 'Cause muthafuckas say they done one minute, and the next, they back together."

"We're done for good. I even gave back the Audi. As bad as it sounds, I never loved Nolen. He didn't give me butterflies like you do, and he damn sure didn't push me to do something different. Our situation was one of pure convenience. Rocco, I left my job and my only security just so I can be with you. If that doesn't show you I care, I don't know what else to do."

Rocco put his head in his hands before finally glancing back at me. "Look, ma, I can't make no guarantees in how this gon' play out. All I can say is that I ain't gon' fight whatever happens."

Just like that, I became putty in his hands once again. I crawled over to Rocco and straddled him. After sliding his shirt over his head, I put soft kisses on his chest. He gripped my butt in his hand and squeezed it gently.

"Hol' up. I got something for you," I panted.

"What you got?" Rocco's smile was wide as hell.

I slid off his lap and grabbed my phone. Once I found what I was looking for, I laid it back on the dresser.

I need a daddy (daddy)
Can you be my daddy (daddy)

"I still owe you for that dance you paid for, daddy." Sliding my shirt over my head, I tossed it on his lap.

"Ah, shit. You wild, ma."

With that sexy ass grin of his, Rocco rested back on his forearms as I began to perform to what was now our theme song.

***

Three days later…

"Can I ask you a question?"

"Wassup?" Rocco briefly glanced my way.

We were on our way to grab something to eat. For the past few days, we'd been glued together, only coming up for air whenever we were hungry or thirsty.

"What do you do for a living?" I asked, and Rocco chuckled. "What's funny?"

"The fact that you just now asking about this."

"It just dawned on me. So what do you do?

"I'm a soul collector," he remarked, and I looked at him like he was crazy. "Nah, I'm just bullshittin' with ya. I flip houses."

"You know what? You play entirely too much. How long

you been doing that?"

"A few years."

"Do you like it?"

"It brings in the money that pays the bills, so I guess it's a'ight."

"I've always been curious about house flipping from watching those shows on HGTV."

"I might have to let you roll with me one day, so you can see how it works."

"I'd like that. What about your family? Are they around?" I asked, and Rocco got this stoic expression on his face. "I'm sorry. Did I hit a sore topic?"

He glanced over at me. "Nah, it's all good. I ain't really got no family. My parents died when I was younger."

"I'm so sorry." *Me and my inquisitive ass.*

Ten minutes later, Rocco pulled up to a restaurant called Eat My Catfish. We both hopped out of the car and made our way to the building.

"Emera? Emera, is that you?" I heard a familiar voice call just as we reached the entrance.

Spinning swiftly on my heels, I faced the person. My mouth fell wide open when I noticed who was running my way. Even though it had been almost six years, I could never forget that face. *What is she doing here?*

"Hot damn! It is you. Come here." She tried to give me a hug, but I stepped away.

"What's the matter? Don't you wanna give your mama a hug?" she asked.

"Nah." I slowly shook my head.

At that moment, it was like everything came rushing back to me. All the days I went without food, the unnecessary beatings, the name calling, and the countless men coming in and out of our house.

"I can't believe I'm seeing you after all this time. When London called and said that you were here, I didn't believe her. I had to come see for myself. Hey, London, here go my baby right here. We ain't gotta go looking for her," Mama said, waving her over.

I was so embarrassed. Not only were her clothes dirty, but her wig was shifted, and she smelled like month-old collard greens.

"Why did you let her come here?" I shouted at Ms. London as soon as she came over.

"Because she wanted to see you, sweetie." Ms. London looked taken aback by the tone of my voice.

"But I asked you not to tell her I was here."

"Hold on one damn minute. Who the hell you think you talking to like that? I didn't raise you to disrespect yo' elders. This is your godmother. Apologize right now," Mama spat.

"It's okay, Ena," Ms. London mumbled.

"Nah, it's not. This little bitch is still disrespectful. Don't think I didn't see you frowning your face. What? You think you better than me? Well, you ain't! As soon as that pussy gets old, he gon' be on to the next. And how you gon' try to frown at somebody when you out here looking like a hoe. Look at them damn shorts all up yo' ass."

"Okay, Ena, I think that's enough."

"Un-un. She been acting this way since she was a little girl. If I would've put my foot in her ass more often, then maybe she'd have some act right. Whew, chile, she don' got my pressure up." Mama took her hand and wiped the sweat beads from her forehead.

"Why the fuck did you come here? You ain't ever been a mother to me, so why try to act like one now? You wanna talk about me. Well, at least I don't look like the walking dead."

Mama hauled off and slapped the shit out of me. After the initial shock wore off, I leaped forward and wrapped my hands around her neck.

"That's the last time you will ever put yo' hands on me!"

Her eyes bulged halfway out her head as I applied pressure. It took Ms. London and Rocco to pull me off her.

"Emera, what is wrong with you! That is your mother," Ms. London fussed.

"She might have given birth to me, but this crackhead ain't my mama!"

I took off running back to the car. After all this time, she still hadn't changed. What mama would say all those hurtful things that she uttered to me?

When Rocco finally made it to the car, I turned and looked out the window. He grabbed my face. "You good?"

"I don't wanna talk about it right now." I sniffled.

"It might make you feel better to get that shit off yo' chest."

"I said I don't want to talk about it!"

Rocco leaned back in his seat, hit the volume on the radio, and pulled off.

***

The next morning when I got up, my head was pounding like crazy. I looked to my right and noticed that Rocco was still asleep. I felt bad about yelling at him yesterday. Truth be told, I was embarrassed by Mama. The way she came at me in front of him was so fucked up.

I tried to ease out of bed, but the movement woke Rocco. He rolled over and glanced at me.

"'Sup?" he spoke.

"Hey. I think I owe—"

"You'on owe me no explanation, ma." He cut me off.

"Even If I don't, I'd still like to get this off my chest."

He nodded and brushed his hand down his face.

"As I'm sure you know by now, that fiend was my mother. I found out about her addiction when I was just five years old. She was shooting up in the bathroom when I caught her."

"Damn. That's fucked up," he uttered while scratching his neck.

"That's not the worst of it. To support her habit, she turned tricks in our apartment, where I laid my head. I can't tell you how many men came through our door. I was always scared, wondering if one of them was going to rape me. On top of that, she used to beat me for any ol' thing. If I looked at her wrong or even sneezed too loud, she would pick up whatever was nearby and whip my ass with it. I never had food or clothes since she spent all the money on drugs. She once told me that I had to go out and get it just like she did if I needed something. My daddy was one of her tricks. He didn't claim me because he didn't want his wife to leave him. So in public, he would pretend like we didn't know each other. Rocco, it was pure hell living there."

Rocco ran his hand down his face again. "So how you end

up here?"

"When I was seventeen, I ran away and didn't look back."

"Just like that? You just up and dipped out?"

"Yup."

"Did you ever tell anybody about what she was doing to you?"

"Nah. Despite how she treated me, I didn't want to see her locked up."

When Rocco stood up, I thought he was going to console me. Instead, he trekked out of the room. *Maybe all my drama is too much for him. I should've just kept my mouth shut.*

***

An hour later, we were riding in Rocco's car, in complete silence. He hadn't said much to me since we left the house. I could see something was weighing heavily on his mind by the way his eyebrows creased.

I hated feeling this feeling of uncertainty. After sharing something so personal, I figured it would bring us closer. Now, I wasn't sure how things would be moving forward. *Is all this too much for him?* That was the one question that kept going through my mind.

"Where are we?" I asked, glancing around. Consumed by my thoughts, I hadn't paid much attention during our drive. I knew we weren't in Fayetteville because of the dirt roads. Rocco never said where we were going. He'd only told me to get dress so we could take a ride.

"We're in Huntsville."

"Huntsville?"

"Yeah," Rocco uttered.

What the hell is in Huntsville?

Huntsville was a small area in the country, located about forty-five minutes from Fayetteville. It was mainly occupied by farmers and people that liked to live off the grid.

Rocco turned down a dirt road that led to an old, wooded house. A horse barn sat off to the right and big bulls behind a fence on the left. The grass was high like it hadn't been cut in weeks, and the big cornfield adjacent to the house gave it a spooky feel.

"Why are we here again?" I asked as Rocco killed the engine.

"C'mon and get out. You'll see once we get in here."
I sucked my teeth and pushed the door open.

The inside of the house didn't look any better than the outside. The furniture was dated with a weird smell, and the walls were all broken up.

"Why did you bring me here?"

Rocco chuckled. "I told you it was something I wanted you to see. Just have a seat, and I'll be right back."

Folding my arms across my breasts, I glared at him. "Do you see that couch? Ain't no telling what's in there. Go ahead and handle your business so we can leave."

"There you go actin' like a brat. I'll be back in just a minute."

"Whatever. You need to hurry up."

Twenty minutes went by, and Rocco still hadn't returned. I was starting to get antsy. *What's taking him so long?*

Just then, a giant ass rat ran across the floor, causing me to leap on the couch.

"Rocco, hurry up! It's a rat in here!" I yelled.

When I heard footsteps coming down the hall, I breathed a sigh of relief.

"It's about tim…" My voice trailed when Rocco entered the room, followed by another person.

"Hello, Emera. It is so nice to see you again after all this time." The person smiled wickedly at me.

I shot my eyes at Rocco. *What the fuck!* My stomach did somersaults as my mind raced out of control.

"Vladir," I mumbled.

"How you doing, sweetheart?"

"Muthafucka, you set me up!" I screamed at Rocco, and he smirked.

Emera

My first instinct was to scream, but I knew that shit wouldn't do any good. Nobody was close enough to even hear me. So my next thought was to figure out a quick escape plan.

"This has been a long time coming," Vladir told Rocco as they dapped each other up.

"No doubt. What you want me to do with the shit that she left at the crib?" He questioned.

"Toss them out, burn 'em, or hell, give them to a lady friend. She won't be needing them."

My hands trembled as I listened to them talk as if I wasn't in the room.

"Cool. I'ma be out. I got som' other business that I need to tend to." When Rocco glanced at me, I became belligerent.

"Why would you do this to me? You let me pour my feelings out, when all along, you were setting me up! I trusted you, Rocco."

"It wasn't personal, ma. Just business." He shrugged.

"Fuck you! Fuck you! I hate you!" I shouted before spitting toward his feet.

Shaking his head, Rocco casually strolled toward the door. My heart crushed even more as I watched him leave.

"Wow! You look just like your mother did when I first met her—so beautiful and full of life. How've you been?" Vladir casually asked as he ran his tongue along his bottom teeth.

Not a lot had changed about him, except his hair had grown out to shoulder length, and he was now rocking a full beard.

"Vladir, please don't kill me. I'm so sorry about what happened!" I pleaded.

"Emera...Emera. You couldn't possibly be sorry after what you did."

"I swear to you, they were just gon' take the money and leave. It was never the plan to kill you. We needed to get away."

"That doesn't fuckin' matter. I looked out for you when your whore of a mother wouldn't. I gave you a job and invited you to my home. Still, after everything I did, you betrayed me. It took me years to locate you. Honestly, I thought that you had gotten away for good. That is until a couple of months ago when I got word that you were here."

I hopped off the chair and took off running. Just as I got to the door, my neck snapped back. I grabbed a statue off the table and swung it wildly. Vladir punched me in the stomach, and I fell on the floor.

"You stupid cunt," he snarled and kicked me in the side.

I balled into the fetal position as he continued the vicious kicks. Once he'd tired himself out, he squatted next to me. Wrapping his hands around my neck, he began to choke me. I gasped for air while clawing at his hands. It felt like he was crushing my windpipe.

When I was just at the point of passing out, he finally released my neck. My throat burned as I attempted to suck in the air.

"Don't you ever try that shit again! Do you hear me?" He gritted, and I nodded vigorously.

"Good. Now I can show you the room you'll be staying in." Vladir snatched me up and tossed me over his shoulder as if I was a rag doll.

My heart raced as he carried me up to a bedroom and threw me on the bed. When I saw the ropes hanging from the poles, I knew this was just the beginning of my nightmare. *Why, Rocco?*

"Please, don't do this." I cried.

My pleas fell on deaf ears as Vladir continued to tie me to the bed. Afterward, he stuck a sock in my mouth.

"Hang here for a while, and I'll be back. Oh… no pun intended," he said with a sadistic chuckle.

Rocco

Three days later…

R occo, please come save me. Don't let him kill me! I love youuuu!

"Argh!" I shot up in the bed and glanced around frantically.

For the second night in a row, I'd had another fucked-up dream. Usually, once a job was completed, I wouldn't think shit else about it. Being brought up in a household where the words *I hate you* were like saying hello had made a nigga shell hard. I had my bitch ass daddy to thank for that. He had never shown love to me. Even the slightest offense would trigger that nigga, sending him into a fit of rage.

Once, he pushed my head under the water and held it there until I passed out. Another time, he made me sleep on the back porch for a night, all because I asked for a dog. On several occasions, he made it known that Ma Dukes should have aborted me. Maybe it wasn't all his fault that he was fucked up. Those drugs had played a big part.

I didn't know how he became an addict, but that nigga was gone. Fucked up part was, my mom never left him, despite the bullshit he put us through. She stuck with that nigga until he ended her life and then took his own.

After that tragedy, shit only got worse for me. I was sent to live with my mom's sister, who only took me in because of the money the state offered her. That bitch treated me like trash. She would often leave me the scraps after dinner or make me take baths in the same dirty water that her nigga used. Let her tell it, she couldn't afford to take on an extra mouth. So I had to get what was left over.

That check I got, my aunt used it all to keep her kids fly and gambled off the rest. Once I turned fifteen, I finally got tired of her shit and bounced. For a few months, I hopped from place to place until one of my boys, Santino, put me on to Vladir.

Things looked up for a nigga from that point. Vladir made me one of his debt collectors. What that meant was that I had to collect his paper from people that owed him. If they didn't have the money, I handled them accordingly.

On rare occasions, he had me make drops at meat plants, funeral homes, and airports. Back then, and even to this day, I had no idea what Vladir did for a living. He never volunteered that info, and I never asked. As long as I got my paper, nothing else mattered.

Vladir had always fucked with a nigga the long way. That was why my loyalty to him trumped whatever me and shawty had going on.

After checking my phone for the time, I got down on the floor to do a few pushups.

"One… two… three."

I left my job and security for you.

"Four... five... six... seven..."

He didn't give me butterflies like you do.

"Fifteen... sixteen..."

I think I'm falling in love with you.

"Fuck!" *Why can't I get that grimy bitch out of my head?*

That broad wasn't to be trusted. She was the type that would fuck you good right before she slit yo' throat. Hell, she'd set my nigga Vladir up when he was just trying to help her. What would make me any different?

I pushed myself up one last time and got back into the bed. Using the lightning from the storm as a distraction, I tried to focus on something else. The shit was tough, especially with the scent of her perfume stuck on my pillows. Just thinking about that shit gave a nigga visuals of the last time I was in between her thighs. *This ain't your situation. Whatever she is going through, she deserved that shit. You definitely can't trust her. She just a money-hungry broad.*

After tossing and turning for the next thirty minutes, I was finally able to close my eyes. That shit didn't last long because my cell started going off. I rolled over and snatched it up.

"Yeah?"

"Come to the house now. I need you to keep an eye on her while I go handle some business."

Damn! Why the fuck can't you handle this shit by yourself? I did my part.

"A'ight. Give me like an hour, and I'll be there," I finally responded and ended the call.

***

It had been about thirty minutes since I made it back to the house. Vladir told me he would only be gone for about an hour or two. I didn't know what that nigga had up or how long he planned to keep shawty here. All I knew was after this visit, I was done. The quicker I distanced myself from this shit, the quicker I could get on with my life.

Thump! All of a sudden, I heard a loud, crashing noise.

Fuck is she doing? I quickly sprung to my feet and headed upstairs.

Along with the sound of muffled cries, I could also hear movement. I stood at the door for a minute, debating if I should go in. The sound of something else crashing pressed me forward. I pushed the door open and ran inside. Somehow, shawty had managed to untie one of her hands, but the rest of her body was still bound. The noise I'd heard was from a lamp that fell over.

"What the hell you doing?" I bellowed.

"Mmm-mmm," she mumbled.

"What?"

"Mmm-mmm."

I took the sock out of her mouth.

"Get the fuck away from me!" she shouted.

I ignored her rant and slid her body back onto the bed. Suddenly, the strong scent of piss hit my nostrils. Judging by the big ring on the sheet, shawty had pissed on herself a few times.

"Yo, what the fuck. How long you been laying in this shit?" I asked.

"What difference does it fuckin' make? You left me here to endure this abuse!"

"You right. It don't matter."

I grabbed her arm to put the rope back on it, and she winced in pain.

"Sss!"

"What now!" I sighed as my eyes went to her wrist. There was a deep laceration from where the rope had dug into her skin, causing it to bleed. "You in here trying to escape and gon' end up killing yourself."

"Fuck you!" She leaned forward and spit on me. The glob of spit landed on my face.

I wrapped my hands around her neck and pushed her back on the bed. "Don't you ever do that shit…"

"Just go ahead and kill me. It's been days since I last ate, my body is numb, and I can't feel my legs. I don't want to suffer like this anymore. Please, just take me out of my misery, Rocco," she cried.

There it was, that fuckin' tugging at my heart again. I released her neck and stood up. Turning for the door, I stomped out and went back downstairs. This wasn't the first time her words had gotten to a nigga. The first time was when she confessed her feelings for me. The second time was when she told me about her upbringing. Seeing that our pasts mirrored each other's had a nigga feeling slighted.

At that moment, I knew I had a decision to make: go ahead and end the job or sabotage everything by getting caught up. The choice had come easier than I thought.

Ten minutes later, I crept back into the room with a packet of peanut butter crackers and a cup of water. I tried to place a cracker in her mouth. Stubbornly, she turned her head the other way.

"Eat the damn cracker!" I barked.

Emera shot me a death stare before opening her mouth. Once she munched that one down, I gave her another one. In less than a minute, her ass had eaten all the crackers. I put the cup of water to her lips, and she lapped that shit up like a dog.

"You good?" I asked, and she rolled her eyes.

"Look, you might not believe me, but this situation wasn't personal. I had a job to do." For some reason, I felt compelled to explain myself.

Out of nowhere, she started laughing hysterically.

"What the hell is funny?" I frowned.

"You."

"What about me?"

"You have feelings for me, but you don't want to admit it."

"Yo, you delusional as fuck. Ain't no way I would seriously fall for a grimy hoe like you."

"If that's true, then why are you getting so angry?"

"Think what you wanna think. I know what it is."

"Silly Rocco. You still trying to convince yourself that what we had wasn't real. Look at you, all in your feelings 'cause you don' fucked around and fell for a stripper. All those barriers you put up, I broke right through 'em. Now you're mad at yourself for allowing it to happen," she asserted.

"Man, fuck all this. I ain't finna listen to this bullshit!" I snatched the sock up and stuffed it back into her mouth. "You got shit all wrong. I don't give a damn about you. That's why I'm leaving yo' ass right here."

By the time I made it back downstairs, Vladir was coming through the door. I glanced at the person with him. *What the fuck is she doing here? This nigga is on som' other shit.*

Emera

"**G**o ahead, get in there!" I heard Vladir belt at someone.

My eyes bucked when I saw Mama stumble into the room, wearing an old, ripped dress that was two sizes too big for her. The glossy gaze in her eyes was a clear sign that she was high as a kite.

"Emera, look, we have a visitor."

"Mmm," I mumbled.

Mama's beady eyes shifted back and forth between me and Vladir.

"What the hell are you doing with my daughter? I thought you brought me here so we can handle business?"

"You don't know?"

"Know what?" Mama hissed and put her hands on her boney hips.

"Your daughter set me up to get robbed almost six years ago."

"Hell nah! She wouldn't do nothing like that."

"Tell her, Emera."

How the fuck can I tell her, and my mouth is gagged?

"Mmm-mmm."

"Well damn. So the stories I heard back then were true. Hmm." Mama started scratching all over.

It pained me to see all those sores on her. Her arms looked as if Freddy Krueger had clawed her up.

"Em, is that why you ran away?" she asked, and my eyes bucked. She was holding a casual conversation as if I wasn't tied to this bed.

"Mmm, mmm, mmm!"

"What? I can't hear you. Can you take that thing off her? I can't understand what she saying," Mama turned to Vladir and said.

Even he looked confused by her unusual response to the situation.

"Nope. We got things to discuss."

"Well, can I get my money first?" She stuck out her thin hand while eyeing him down.

What the hell was wrong with her? She was worried about money while I was being held hostage. Vladir started to laugh. He then took his fist and rammed it into Mama's face. Her skinny neck snapped back, and blood gushed from her nose. Vladir grabbed her by the neck and started choking her.

I watched in horror as he lifted her in the air like a madman. She was clawing and scratching his hands.

"You're so fuckin' pathetic and a waste of human life. You see what she's worried about, huh? Fuckin' money! She doesn't care anything about you. I tried to save you from this, but you betrayed me instead."

With each word that fell from his lips, the grip on mama's neck just got tighter. Her eyes were bulging out of their sockets as her tongue literally hung from her mouth.

"Mmm, mmm, mmm," I mumbled.

No matter how shitty of a mother she'd been, I still didn't want to see her die.

When her body suddenly went limp, I knew that she was dead. I laid there crying my eyes out as Vladir dropped her like she was a piece of trash. Without uttering a word, he stepped over her body and slammed the door on the way out. How could someone be so heartless as to kill a mother in front of their daughter?

***

A few hours later…

My eyes fluttered when I felt my body lift into the air. I started swinging my arms wildly.

"Chill, ma. It's just me," I heard Rocco whisper.

When my eyes finally settled, I realized that it was him for real. *What is he doing?* I glanced around and saw that we were in a bathroom. I moved my lips, suddenly realizing that I wasn't gagged anymore.

"What are you doing?" I whispered.

"I'ma let you take a quick bath, and then you can put on these clothes I brought you from the crib."

Rocco tried to put me on my feet, but my legs gave out. He caught me right before I fell into the wall.

"I can't stand up. My legs are weak."

Rocco sat me on the toilet and removed my clothes. Once

he was done, he put me in the old tub, which was barely filled with water.

"Hurry and clean yourself," he instructed after passing me a towel.

"Rocco, wait!"

"'Sup?"

"Why are you doing this?"

"To be honest, I don't know."

"Wait," I called again.

"What?" His tone was snappy.

"Is... Is my mama dead?"

"Get cleaned up," was all he told me.

I broke down crying when he left the bathroom. Just knowing I'd caused her death made my heart throb. She didn't deserve to die like that.

"Why, God!" I sobbed.

It was becoming painfully clear just how sadistic Vladir was. One thing was sure; I'd fucked with the wrong person.

Twenty minutes later, Rocco entered the bathroom, wearing a blank expression. My eyes roamed his body as I silently took him in. As usual, he was dressed suavely in Gucci from head to toe.

"Get out," he demanded.

"I need a little bit longer."

"Nope, it's time to go. You should've been using your time wisely instead of sitting in here crying over shit that can't be changed."

"How can you be this damn cold? I lost my fuckin' mama,

don't you care?"

"Nah, I don't. Get your ass out before I drag you out."

"I hate you!"

Rocco trekked over and pulled me from the tub. I swung my arm to hit him, and he smacked it away. We began to grapple.

"I hate you! I hate you!" I snarled, throwing vicious blows at him.

"Calm the fuck down!" he gritted.

I slapped him, and he pushed me into the sink. When I tried to stand up, Rocco put his force against me. Before I knew it, my legs were spread wide like a pair of scissors, and Rocco had stuffed himself inside of me. When the hardness of his rod met my wetness, I threw my arms around his neck.

"I hate you," I uttered while throwing it on him.

His strokes were rough yet gentle. I dug my nails into his back.

"Mmm." An involuntary moan escaped my lips.

Rocco roughly put kisses on my neck, sending chills shooting down my spine.

Even in the thick of things, my love for this man remained strong. Why was that? He'd betrayed me in the worst way. Yet, I couldn't find a way to hate him even when I wanted to. *Maybe I'm the crazy one.*

"Argh, fuck!" He suddenly gritted when his semen shot inside of me.

By now, we were both panting like dogs as we collapsed on the floor.

Rocco closed his eyes for a brief moment, and I used that as an opportunity to make my move. Shooting to my feet, I raced at full speed down the hall. I felt this surge of happiness shoot all over when I made it to the front door. My freedom was literally on the other side of that wall.

"This is why I can't trust yo' ass," Rocco bellowed just as I grabbed the knob.

"You can't take me back in there. He's going to kill me."

Rocco grabbed me in his arms and carried me back to the room.

"Get dressed, right now!" He threw a pile of clothes at me.

Hot tears slid down my cheeks as I began to put the clothes on. After I was done dressing, he tied me back to the bed.

"Where is my mom?" I asked. It had just dawned on me that she wasn't here. "Where is she?" I yelled.

He shot his eyes at me but remained silent.

"I neeeeed to know. Don't leave me, he—"

He stuffed the sock back in my mouth and marched out the room. At that moment, I felt defeated. I'd probably just ruined the only chance to get out of here. *Shit!*

Rocco

Two days later…

"**I**'m thinking about heading back to Oklahoma tomorrow. The job is done, so ain't no reason for me to stick around," I explained to Vladir.

Being around shawty had clouded my judgment like a motherfucker. A nigga was doing shit I wouldn't typically do, which lead to questions of my loyalty.

"I agree. We'll be leaving here soon anyway," he stated.

"Let me ask you som'."

"Shoot."

"What you plan on doing to her?"

Vladir sipped from his Styrofoam cup before placing it on the table. "Good question. Before seeing her again, I was so sure I wanted to kill her. Now, not so much. I think I've had a change of heart."

"If you ain't gon' kill her, what's the plan?"

"Well, I was thinking about grooming her."

"Grooming her for what?" I was confused by this shit.

"To be my wife," he revealed.

I looked at this fool sideways before I busted out laughing. "You jokin', right?"

"Hear me out. That smut convinced her to set me up, which meant she was loyal to him. Just as she was loyal to you when it appeared, you two would be together. With the right coaching, I can have her eating out the palm of my hand. Most broads are like puppies. All you gotta do is feed and pet them, and you'll have a loyal bitch for life."

I bit the inside of my jaw while glaring at him. "Do you, man."

"I will, and if she's not willing to comply—eh, I guess I'll just sell her to the highest bidder. No need to discard her when she can bring me in a lot of money. I'm sure you can attest to this... that bitch is nesting a golden goose egg between those sweet thighs."

"I'll get up with you later," I grumbled.

"Are you good? You suddenly seem upset about something," he asked with a small
smirk.

I gritted my teeth.

"I'm straight. Just got som' shit on my mind."

"Do me a favor before you leave town," Vladir said.

"'Sup?"

"It's a guy who owes me money. I need you to go collect it. He'll already be expecting you."

"A'ight, shoot me a text with the info. What you want me to do with the money?"

"Keep it. Consider it a bonus for all the hard work you've

done."

"Shit, that's cool right there. Good looking out."

"No thanks needed."

I threw Vladir a head nod on my way out.

As I pulled off, a nigga got to thinking hard. Was I making the right decision? Did I want shit to end like this? Could Vladir actually be serious? A part of me knew this was the right move, yet the other part held reservations. *Just let her go, Roc. You can't trust her. Remember what happened when you tried to help?*

Thankfully, the text from Vladir finally came through. It was just the confirmation I needed to keep it moving.

An hour later, I pulled in front of a red shotgun house off 15th Street. Unlike the rest of Fayetteville, this area looked like shit. Most of the homes were either rundown or completely boarded up, and it was trash strewn over the streets.

"Rocco, right?" A tall, light-skinned dude peeked his head through the screenless door just as I approached the porch.

"Yeah. You got that for me?" I looked at him before glancing around to scope out my surroundings.

In an unfamiliar neighborhood, I always made sure to watch my back. I never knew who was plotting.

"It's all there. Tell Vladir I said good looking out."

"I gotcha," I told him and slid the money into my pocket.

"'Preciate it."

I was on my way back to the whip when an old, dirty fiend approached me.

"Say, man, you got anything on you?"

"Nah, I ain't got nothing." I cracked my door open, ready

to hop inside.

"C'mon, I know you got something. I'on care what it is."

I glanced at his yellow, rotten teeth and frowned.

"Look, dawg, I told you I ain't got nothing. Back the fuck out of my face!" I barked.

"I bet this pistol will make you come up out of them pockets." He whipped out a gun and trained it on me.

I gut-punched his ass before jumping into my car. When he grabbed ahold of my door, I slammed it on his arm.

"Argh, fuck!" he grunted.

He dropped the pistol, and it hit the floorboard. I used my free hand to reach for it. *Pow! Pow! Pow!* Suddenly, a barrage of shots went off. I peeked into the rearview mirror and spotted ol' boy running from the house.

"Get that nigga! Vladir said that we can't let him get away!"

What the fuck! His bitch ass set me up.

"Oh shit, my arm!" The fiend's voice went about two octaves higher when I peeled off. I dragged him about a good fifty feet before releasing the door.

Pow! Pow! Pow! Pow! More shots hit the whip as I zipped down the street and bent the corner. Snatching up my phone, I punched in a number and waited for an answer.

"Look who finally—"

"Fuck the small talk, nigga. I need you to do me a favor."

Emera

I was jolted out of my sleep when icy-cold water splashed on me. My eyes frantically moved about the room. Vladir was standing over me with a gun and some big white guy that I'd never seen before.

"Look at your filthy ass laying there covered in piss and shit. You fuckin' disgust me!" Vladir snarled while giving me the look of death.

What the hell was I supposed to do? You basically left me here to rot.

"I guess you didn't think I would find out, huh?" he barked.

I didn't know what the fuck he was talking about. To be honest, I couldn't even begin to think. Not only was I freezing cold, but it felt like I was paralyzed. Since I'd been tied to this bed for days, I'd long ago lost blood circulation. Everything from my arms to my toes was stiff.

"So, you don't hear me talking to you?" He snatched the sock out of my mouth.

"I don't know what you're talking about."

Vladir let out a hearty chuckle. He then turned his back and moseyed over to the dresser. When he came back, I noticed this weird instrument thing in his hand. He raised my shirt, and a loud gasp escaped my lips.

"Emera, I'm gonna teach you a little lesson for your betrayal."

"I didn't do anything! What are you talking about?"

"Maybe this will refresh your memory."

Vladir took that thing and clamped it on my nipple.

"Ahhhhhhhhh!" I yelled at the top of my lungs.

It felt like someone was biting me. He squeezed down harder until blood squirted on him.

"Noooooo! Please stoppppppp!"

Violently, my body jerked back and forth.

"You ready to come clean yet?"

I couldn't even reply because of all the pain. After about a minute, he finally removed the clamp. Due to the numbness in my nipple, I could no longer feel it.

"Are you ready to come clean?"

"I don't—"

He put the clamp on my other nipple.

"Ahhhhhhhh!" I was crying, and this sick fool was laughing. He finally removed it and glared at me.

"You know I could've killed you, right?"

He was so close I could feel the hotness of his breath on my face.

"The only reason I've allowed you to continue breathing is because I've always had a soft spot for you. But you've disappointed me yet again. Do you want to know how?"

Is this a trick question? "H-Ho-How," I whimpered.

"By fucking him in *my house*! He literally dumped his seeds in your womb and tied you back to the bed. How stupid can you be? Just like that other trash you were with, Rocco used you. Think about it. If he actually cared, wouldn't he have taken you with him?"

The reality slapped me hard in the face. As much as I hated to admit it, Vladir was right. Rocco had definitely used me again.

"I'm sorry. I promise it won't happen again. Just don't kill me," I pleaded.

"You hear this? She says she's sorry." Vladir turned to the big, white man standing there with a blank expression and his hands folded.

"I wanna believe you, Emera. I really do. The thing is, you haven't given me a reason to trust your word. So the only way to be sure you won't betray me again is to punish you."

Tears poured out of my eyes. "I'm sorry. Whatever you want me to do, I'll do it."

"Of course you will. Take her to the bathroom and do what we discussed," he told the guy once he'd removed the ropes.

By now, my eyes were damn near bulging out of my head. *What the hell did they discuss? Is he going to kill me?* So many thoughts went through my head at that moment.

"Don't look so afraid. The good news is that you're not going to die—right now. The bad news is that you will feel severe pain. Oh, just so you know. I took care of your little boyfriend. You won't be seeing him around here ever again."

A single tear fell down my cheek as I thought about Rocco being dead. *Is that why he hadn't been around?* I hated to think that someone else was killed because of me.

As soon as Vladir moved out the way, the guy snatched me up and carried me to the bathroom. After forcing me to strip out of my clothes, he ordered me inside the bathtub next. I was scared for my life when I noticed the boiling hot water. You could literally see the steam rolling off it.

"Please don't make me get in that!" I pleaded.

Without uttering a word, he scooped me up and tossed me in the water.

"Arrrrgh!" I screamed at the top of my lungs.

"Clean up now!" he roared.

***

An hour later, I was back in the room, waiting for Vladir. After damn near having my skin melted off, I was forced to put on a skintight black skirt, fishnet top, and peep-toe heels.

Even though I'd worn skimpier shit than this before, I felt so uncomfortable. Small blisters had formed on my legs and arms from the scolding water. *God, if you're real, please get me out of this. I promise to straighten my life. I will never do anything to get myself in another situation.*

No sooner than I finished my prayer, I heard what sounded like a car outside. *Maybe that's Rocco.* I know Vladir said he'd killed him, but just maybe he was lying.

Easing off the bed, I gently tiptoed to the window. When I noticed a familiar car, my eyebrows drew into a straight line. *Is that who I think it is?* I watched closely as the door to the Lincoln flew open.

"Why the fuck are you here?" Vladir snarled while meeting the person halfway.

"Where is my money? You told me I would have it in two days. It's been almost two weeks, and I have yet to get it. If you don't give me what you owe me right now, you will regret it."

"Who the hell do you think you're talking to?" Vladir snarled while stepping closer.

"Muthafucka, I'm talking to yo' ass. I could've kept that bitch for myself and made more money. Hell, if it wasn't for me getting that tip, you wouldn't have ever known where to find her. So the way I see it, you owe me double of what we first agreed on. And if I don't get it, I might have to pay that old lady a visit. I'm sure she would love to hear that her goddaughter didn't actually skip town," Mont threatened.

"Huh!" I gasped while covering my mouth with my hand.

I knew I couldn't trust him. I swear it seemed like everybody around me was a snake.

Pow! My thoughts were suddenly interrupted. I glanced down just as Mont's body hit the ground. "What the fuck!"

Unexpectedly, Vladir glanced up and waved at me with a sinister smile. It was at that moment I knew I was going to die. This man was beyond deranged.

Rocco

"**Y**o, fam, what the fuck is going on? Who you beefin' with?" my boy, Santino, asked.

After letting him know that I had an emergency, he'd made the three-and-a-half-hour drive to see what was up. I had him meet me down by the casino in Siloam Springs. It wasn't safe for me to go back to the crib. That would have been the first place Vladir checked.

"Vladir," I finally revealed, and Santino's eyes widened.

"On the real?" he asked, and I nodded.

Santino scratched the side of his head. "Dawg, you know I've always had your back no matter what it was. But I'on know about this situation. That nigga Vladir ain't wrapped too tight."

I expected that to be his response. Being as though we both worked for Vladir, we were aware of how he got down. There were several instances when we witnessed him strangle grown ass men with his bare hands. Once, he'd beheaded a cat over five hundred dollars.

I wasn't a bitch by a long shot, but even I knew going up against this nigga was going to be a challenge. Regardless, I had to handle my business. I had been loyal to dude, and he put a hit on me.

"Look, man, you know I wouldn't ask you this if I didn't really need you."

"What he do?" Santino questioned.

Starting from the very beginning, I ran the events of the past couple of months down to Santino. I even told him about the feelings that I had for Emera. Not wanting to blindside him, I had to keep it all the way one hunid.

By the time I finally finished, he was just standing there with a blank expression.

"So you in or what?" I asked.

"Even though this shit is crazy as hell, I got your back. I just hope ol' girl is worth all the trouble you about to go through."

"Keeping it real with ya, shawty is worth a couple of bullets. But it ain't just about her. That nigga Vladir gotta see me for the stunt he pulled."

"I feel ya, homie. That shit was foul as hell. So what's the plan?" he asked.

"Hop in the car, and I'll explain everything."

***

An hour later…

Just as we hit the dirt road leading to Vladir's hideout, I spotted his Phantom heading in our direction. *Shit!*

"Ain't that the nigga's whip right there?" Santino asked.

"Yeah, that's him." My eyes turned into slits as my foot slowly pressed down on the gas.

"Yo, kinfolk, what you plan on doing?"

"Change of plans. Since we can't sneak up on this nigga. We just gotta take him head-on."

"Say, man, slow the fuck down. We didn't discuss this shit."

"Everything ain't gon' always go as planned. Sometimes you just gotta roll with the punches as they come."

Santino started bitching and complaining about how fast I was going. I paid his ass no attention as I kept my eyes on Vladir. At this point, we were only a few yards from each other. If one of us didn't turn off, we were bound to hit in a head on collision.

"Yo, Rocco, what the fuck is you doing? Slow this mufucka down!" Santino barked. "Ah shit... Ah shit! We 'bout to crash!" Santino yelled.

Just as we came within a foot of crashing into Vladir's car, it suddenly jerked to the left and plowed into a trailer. I slammed on the brakes and glanced in my rearview mirror. When I didn't see any movement signs, I reached underneath my seat and gripped my pistol.

"Shit! I think I got whiplash," Santino griped.

"Quit fuckin' whinin', nigga. We gotta handle these mufuckas!" I spat while throwing my door open.

I was ready to step out when two shots came flying through the front window. *Pow! Pow!*

With our pistols already locked and loaded, me and Santino hopped out. We didn't hesitate to start busting. The big nigga firing at us took one shot to the shoulder.

"Yo, cover me, dawg. I gotta go get this nigga Vladir."

"I gotcha," Santino told me. "Argh shit!"

As soon as he said that, a bullet hit him in the leg.

"Fuck!" I mumbled.

"I'm good. I'm good. Go handle your business." He waved me off.

Santino suddenly got this deranged look on his face. He started spraying bullets everywhere. By the time his clip was empty, the big dude was laying facedown.

I crept up on the side of Vladir's whip and peeked in the window.

"Oh shit! Emera!"

I started to panic when I noticed her eyes closed and tiny trails of blood dripping down her forehead. I snatched the door open and gently lifted her from the car. Shawty's eyes fluttered open.

"Rocco? You're alive," she whispered.

"Yeah, I'm good, ma."

She smiled weakly while throwing her arm around my neck. "I had a dream that you were going to save me."

I didn't know how to feel when she put a kiss on my lips.

"Get me out of here," she finally said.

My blood began to boil as I carried her over to my car. There were several bruises on her body, and her left eye was black.

"Say, we gotta raise up. I see a truck driving this way," Santino urged.

After sliding Emera in the backseat of the whip, I stood up and faced the black truck.

"What you doin', dawg?" Rocco queried.

"I ain't running from this nigga. We 'bout to face up."

"Nigga, you just insist on dying today, don't you?" Santino uttered.

"No, Rocco. Let's just leave before he kills us," Emera cried.

I cut my eyes at her and saw the tears streaming down her cheeks. Shawty was scared out of her mind. At that point, I was torn. If I didn't kill this nigga now, we would forever be looking over our shoulders. But if I stayed around, I took the risk of Emera getting hurt.

"Please!" she begged while gazing into my eyes.

With that look on her face, it made my decision easier. I hopped into my whip just as Vladir came to a stop right in front of us. When I saw him hop out with this big machine gun, I mashed my foot on the gas.

Tat! Tat! Tat!

"Ahhh!" Emera screamed. I slid my pistol to Santino, who immediately started busting
out the window.

"Put yo' head down!" I yelled at Emera.

Emera

Two weeks later…

"**G**et away from me!" I swung my hands wildly while trying to get Vladir off me.

"Emera."

"Please don't kill me!"

"Aye, Emera. Wake up. You havin' another nightmare," I heard Rocco say.

My eyes popped open.

"It's just me, ma. You safe," he told me.

When my eyes finally focused, I threw my arms around Rocco's neck and hugged him tightly. "I'm so happy, it's you. That dream felt so real this time."

"You sweatin' bad as hell. C'mon, let's go get in the shower."

I got out of bed and followed Rocco into the bathroom.

While he got the shower ready, I took my nightgown off and tossed it on the floor.

Rocco picked me up and placed me in the tub. Almost instantly, my body felt relaxed. Rocco grabbed the loofah and body wash. Starting at my back, he began to clean my body with delicacy. By the time he made it around to my front side, I felt a thousand times better. This shower was just what I needed to calm my nerves.

Ten minutes later, Rocco cut the water off and wrapped a towel around my body. He then scooped me in his arms and carried me back to the room.

"Rocco, you don't have to keep doing this. I'm able to dress and bathe myself."

Ever since the day he rescued me from Vladir, he'd been handling me as if I were a baby. He wouldn't allow me to do anything unless he was right there with me.

"We already had this conversation, and what I tell you?"

"I know what you said, but all this isn't necessary. Look, I know you feel guilty about what happened. I get that, but it's nothing we can do to change the situation. I forgive you, Rocco. You just gotta forgive yourself."

Rocco continued to dress me like I hadn't said shit. I let out a frustrated breath. *Lord knows I love this man, but he is getting on my damn nerves.*

Knock! Knock!

"Come in," Rocco said.

Santino opened the door and swaggered into the room. I was so thankful because I didn't know how much more I could take of Rocco. Hopefully, Santino would be able to distract him for a minute while I cleared my head.

"'Sup, Emera."

"Hey, Santino," I mumbled.

Santino was about five feet ten, a hundred and eighty pounds with a dark-brown complexion, a diamond grill, and hella tattoos all over his arms and neck. He was funny as shit with a laid-back personality.

Santino peered over at Rocco, sliding on my socks, and shook his head.

"Say, dawg, can I holla at you for a minute."

"What is it?"

"No offense, Emera, but this is kind of private."

"Say no more. He's all yours." I jumped off Rocco's lap and skipped to the door.

Santino chuckled as he stepped out the way.

"Say, man, don't leave out of here. If you wanna get out, then I'll take you when I'm done hollering at him." Rocco instructed.

This shit is ridiculous. "Yeah, okay."

A few minutes later, I was sprawled out on the couch sipping on my fruit juice. The TV was on an old rerun of *Girlfriends*, but I wasn't paying much attention. My thoughts were on my mama. I still couldn't believe that she was gone.

What saddened me most was that we never got the chance to mend our broken relationship. Hell, I couldn't even give her a proper burial because I didn't know where her body was. I wished she had never come back with Vladir. Even more, I wished that she wouldn't have been on drugs. Maybe then, she would have been able to use her brain.

The sounds of voices right outside the window broke through my thoughts. Even though Rocco told me not to leave, curiosity got the best of me. It had been forever since I mingled with people other than Rocco and Santino.

Rocco had us locked away at the Residence Inn in Maryland Heights, a small city outside of St. Louis. He didn't think staying in Fayetteville would be a good idea. That was one thing I agreed with him on.

As soon as I opened the door, I noticed this tall, dark-skinned dude talking with a short, butch looking girl. They both stopped mid-conversation when they saw me standing there.

"'Sup, shawty?" the man finally spoke.

"Hey." I waved.

"Baby thicker than a Snickers," the stud mumbled, and ol' boy dapped her up.

All I did was laugh as I stepped further outside. The cool breeze blowing on my face felt good.

"Say, what's your name?" the guy questioned.

"Emera."

"Oh yeah? I like that. You smoke, Emera?"

I was ready to reply when I heard Rocco's deep voice behind me. "Fuck you think you doing? Huh? Didn't I tell yo' ass not to leave? You hardheaded, man." He was talking to me as if he were my daddy.

"Damn, dawg. Why don't you ease up on her? She wasn't doing nothing."

"Nigga, who the fuck you think you talking to!"

"Obviously, a bitch boy that's mad he can't keep his gal on a leash!" The dude bucked up at him.

"Fuck you say, my nigga?" Rocco snarled.

Oh shit! This is about to go left real quick.

Rocco

I walked up on that nigga and threw a blow to his temple, momentarily dazing him. After catching his footing, he countered back with a jab that missed my jaw by an inch.

"Ol' bitch ass nigga!" he bellowed.

At that point, I was ready to go in on this fool. Snatching off my white tee, I charged at him.

"Yo, Roc, it ain't even worth it. We got bigger shit to deal with," Santino said, grabbing me back. Emera ran over and wrapped her arms around my waist.

I glanced around, realizing that a small crowd had formed. Maybe it was a good thing they'd stopped me. Otherwise, I would've made the stupid mistake of catching a body in broad daylight.

I mean-mugged the shit out of ol' boy before putting my focus on Emera.

"Get yo' ass back inside right now."

She stomped away like somebody had stolen her toy. A nigga didn't give a damn about that. We were on the run, and her ass was out here fraternizing.

"Can you please explain why you would take yo' ass out there when I specifically asked you not to?" I asked once I made it inside the house.

"Because I got tired of sitting in this room. I was suffocating in here."

"I told you I was gonna take you out once I finished. All you had to do was wait a little while longer. What if that nigga had been on some sneak shit? You don't know him or that bitch!" I piped. She was pissing me off, acting like a damn child.

"That's just it. I didn't wanna wait for you to take me out. I wanted to be able to get out by myself."

I pinched the bridge of my nose while glaring at her. "You obviously don't know what we up against, do you?"

"I'm aware, Rocco. The thing is, you're making me feel like I'm back at that house. I can't even go outside without you breathing down my back. Shit is exhausting."

"Let me get this straight. You comparing me looking out for you to the shit that nigga did?"

"Yes, that's exactly what it feels like. I just need you to ease up some."

I slowly nodded my head. "Say less!"

When I strolled off, Emera ran over and grabbed my arm.

"Rocco, wait."

I jerked away from her.

"I needed you to know how I felt so it wouldn't keep being an issue."

It didn't dawn on me just how much I loved her little ass until just a minute ago. Granted, I was stressing about Vladir, but that wasn't the main reason I was so angry. Seeing that nigga standing in her face made me snap. That situation was a clear reminder of why I couldn't be with her.

"Don't even worry 'bout it. I'ma leave for a minute. Once I get back, I'll hit you with some ends, and you can move around."

"What are you talking about?"

"This ain't gon' work, ma. When I'm around you, I can't seem to focus. My head be all fucked up and shit. You take me off my square, and I don't like feeling like this. You get my drift?"

"No, I don't. Why can't you just keep it real with yourself? You have feelings for me, but you don't wanna let yourself go there. You're afraid that I will hurt you."

"You'on know what the fuck you talkin' 'bout."

"Why are you frontin'? Just admit it, Rocco. You love me, don't you? That same look that I saw in your eyes outside was the same one I saw back at the house."

"I'm out, man. You talkin' crazy right now."

"Just be honest," I heard her say as I stepped out the door.

"Everything cool?" Santino questioned.

"Yeah, everything is straight. Let's be out."

***

Later that night, when I made it back to the room, I noticed Emera sprawled across the bed.

"Hey. Where you been?" Her face lit up like a kid in a candy store.

"I had to handle a few things," I told her while sticking my hand into my pocket.

Pulling out a fat knot, I peeled off two Gs and tried to hand it to her.

"I'm not taking that money." She frowned.

"C'mon, shawty. Don't start tripping. Take the money."

"I don't want it." She pushed my hand away.

"Why not?"

"If I take that money, you'll think I'm cool with this, and I'm not. I don't care what you say. I'm not leaving you."

I brushed my hand down my face. "This shit ain't gon' ever work, shawty. I don't trust you, and I know you don't trust me. Our situation is too messy for us to even think about having something real. Besides that, I got this beef with Vladir. I'm too focused on him to give you the attention you need."

"I'm not sure what made you afraid to love, but I'm telling you that I'm different. I want to be with you, Rocco." Emera slid off the bed and walked over to me.

When she tried to touch my face, I turned my head the other way. Why couldn't she just take the money and leave? Why did she have to make this shit harder than it already was? I was giving her an escape, yet she refused to take it.

"Are you fuckin' slow? What part of 'this ain't gonna work' don't you understand? You grimy as hell. I could never trust yo' ass. You fucked me while having a nigga. I'm cool on that!"

I tried to take a tougher approach, hoping it would hurt her feelings. Shawty was persistent, though. She stared up into my eyes with this innocent look.

"I know you're still mad at me, but you just gonna have to get over it. I love you, and I know you love me. So we're stuck together."

Emera dropped to her knees, and within a blink of an eye, my dick was stuffed in her mouth. She was gripping it hard and slurping all over the head, making it sensitive. My knees started to buckle when she pushed me all the way in her mouth and started deep-throating me. At the same time, her hand massaged my balls.

"Ah shit!" I grunted.

Where did this bitch come from? She was like cancer. Even with her past at the forefront of my mind, I couldn't seem to shake her.

Ten minutes later, I busted down Emera's throat. She had a nigga feeling like a hoe. All that was missing from this picture was my thumb in my mouth. *This shit is sad. You let this broad knock you off your square.*

"You planned that shit, didn't you?" I finally asked.

She gave me this coy look. "I'on know what you're talkin' about."

"Yeah, a'ight. C'mere." I pulled her up so that she was at eye level with me.

"Wassup?"

"Look, the only way for this to work is if you follow my lead. I know you don't like me keeping tabs on you, but that's how it gotta go until we handle this Vladir shit. Can I trust you to stay out the way?" I asked, and she nodded.

"I'm serious, Emera. This situation is a lot deeper than you think. Me and Santino got word today that it's a price on our heads. That nigga Vladir is crazier than you will ever know."

Emera sighed. "Are we going to die?"

"Not if you do what I tell you to."

"I'm sorry I got you involved. I never knew my past would come back to haunt me like this," she said.

"I'm a grown ass man. I got myself in this when I chose to come back for you. Besides, Vladir made this shit personal when he put out that hit."

"Can you answer me this one question?"

"'Sup?"

"Was all that really a game for you?"

I let out a deep breath while looking her dead in the eyes.

"Nah. It wasn't a game. A nigga actually caught feeling for ya ass, but I knew we couldn't be together because of the situation. Now, answer som' for me."

"Okay."

"What made me you rob Vladir? Was it ol' boy that you were with?"

She was quiet for a minute before finally speaking. "Not initially. I'm the one that went to him with the idea. I thought it would be an easy way for us to come up. At the last minute, I changed my mind. Shark took that as me wanting Vladir. He said if I didn't go through with the plan, he would kill me. It was nothing else I could do."

"That's yo' word?"

"Yes, that's my word. I never wanted anybody to get hurt. All I wanted was to get as far away from my old life as possible," I explained.

"I appreciate you keeping it real. You could've lied and told me ol' boy set all that up, and I wouldn't have ever known. But that shit was gonna remain in the back of my head. Now that I know the truth, I feel I can trust you a little more."

"I had to. Keeping secrets is what got me here. It was time to be honest." She leaned in and put a kiss on my lips.

When I felt my dick rock up, I lifted Emera and carried her over to the bed.

"Come ride him." I instructed while laying on my back.

Emera crawled over and straddled me. With my mans in her hand, she worked her hips around until I was all the way inside.

"Oh, daddy," she cooed while rocking back and forth.

"Shit," I groaned and bit down on my bottom lip.

Undeniably, the girl had some of the best pussy I'd ever been blessed with. Just from the way her walls gripped me, I knew that her body count wasn't high.

"This yo' dick?" I asked, and she nodded.

"Nah, I wanna hear you speak that shit out loud."

"This my dick!" she moaned while bouncing harder.

I wrapped my hands around her small waist and slammed her into me. With her breasts swinging back and forth, she threw her head back.

"Damn, I love you," I accidentally let slip out.

By the time I realized what I'd said, it was too late to take it back. *Oh well. Fuck it!* A nigga wasn't mad because those were my sentiments.

Emera

One month later…

I was in the middle of putting some box braids in my hair when Rocco busted into the room. "What's wrong?"

"Yo', we gotta be out!" he exclaimed.

"Again? How the fuck does he keep finding us?"

We'd gotten word about a week ago that Vladir found our hiding spot. Urgently, we had to pack up and leave. Now here we were, not even a week later, running again. This was all starting to be too much. Of course, I wasn't going to express that to Rocco, as he'd already told me that I could hide, and he'd come back for me. I was trying to be without my man, so I lied as if everything was okay.

"I'on know, but we really ain't got time to figure that out. Santino out front with the whip waiting on us."

"Can I at least finish this braid?"

"Nah. You gon' have to do that it in the car."

I'm so sick of this shit! Why can't he just leave us alone?

After packing up my hair supplies, I went over to my bag and tossed my clothes inside. Rocco had just bought me a few new outfits, underwear, and two pairs of shoes. It wasn't a lot, but it was enough to start off with. All my other clothes were left behind when we first went on the run.

Rocco said once the situation with Vladir was handled, he could get back to work. The only money we had was a few thousand that Rocco had stashed away. I'd offered to use the money I saved, but Rocco wasn't having it. He told me that as my man, it was his duty to make sure we were straight.

"Y'all got everything?" Santino queried as soon as we got into the car.

"We got the important shit."

"A'ight. Bet! We out of here."

When Santino drove off, I glanced out the window. A couple in the distance caught my eyes. They were walking along the trail holding hands. I wondered to myself if that could ever be me and Rocco. With us always on the run, I didn't know if it was possible.

"You good?" Rocco brought me from my thoughts.

"Not really. I want this shit to come to an end."

"Soon enough, ma. Me and Santino working on a few things."

"Yeah, shawty. Shit gon' be back to normal in no time. Just hang in there." Santino glanced at me through the rearview mirror and winked his eye.

"I hope so because this shit is for the birds."

***

A few hours later…

"Say, man, once I get y'all to Kansas City, I think I'ma head back to Oklahoma," Santino told Rocco.

"Dawg, you think that's a good idea?"

"Not really, but I gotta see my shawty. She been blowing me up, wanting to know when I'ma get back."

"Why don't you just send for her to come out here? We can't afford for you to walk into a crossfire before we put our plan in motion."

"That might just work. I never thought about her coming to me. How you think Emera gon' feel? You know, shawty is a lot to handle at times."

"Man, she'll be cool. Lil Ma, don't really be trippin' on much."

"If that's the case, how come you haven't told her about the situation?"

What situation?

"Because," Rocco said and paused.

I could hear him shift in his seat, probably checking to see If I was still sleeping. When he saw that my eyes were closed, he continued to speak.

"Because I'on think I really should tell her."

"Why is that? Don't you think it's better if she finds out from you instead of somebody else?"

What the hell are they talking about?

"Nah, I think I'll just keep that info to myself. She don' been through enough as is." Rocco sighed.

"That's yo' call," Santino mumbled.

The fact that Rocco was still keeping secrets didn't sit well with my spirit. He was aware of my situation, yet he chose to hide shit. One thing was for sure, I was going to find out what the hell was going on.

***

"Say man, what's with this attitude?"

"I'on know. I just feel moody. Maybe my period is about to come on," I lied.

"C'mere. I'll rub yo' stomach," he offered.

It was actually cute to hear him say that. Still, I wasn't ready to drop my attitude. After all, we'd been through, and Rocco didn't want to keep it one hundred with me.

Rolling my eyes into my head, I sighed. "I'm good. I just wanna lay down."

When I tried to get into the bed, Rocco grabbed my arm.

"What?" I snapped.

"Give me a kiss," he said, and I frowned.

"Stop playing. I ain't in the mood right now."

"So you ain't gon' give your man a kiss?"

"No. I'on feel like that right now."

At this point, I was pissed. The more I mulled over the situation, the more I questioned Rocco's motive. He'd moved us to Kansas, in the middle of nowhere. So once again, I was at his mercy without anyone to turn to if shit popped off.

"A'ight. Since you wanna act like that, I'll keep what I got to myself."

"Whatcha talkin' 'bout?" I lifted a brow.
"I had something for you, but since you acti—"

"What is it?"

"Nah, don't even worry 'bout it. Lay yo bobble-headed ass down if that's what you wanna do."

"C'mon. What is it, baby?"

"Oh, so now I'm yo' baby?" he retorted.

"You know you are," I said, and he smirked.

Suddenly, I heard something moving on the other side of the room. Panic-stricken, I clutched Rocco's shirt.

"What is that?"

"I'on know. Stay right here," he uttered as he tipped over to the closest's door.

"Wait, Rocco. It could be a setup."

"It's cool." He glanced back at me.

By now, my heart was pumping out of my chest.

"Fuck is this?"

"What?" I was craning my neck to see what was inside, but Rocco was blocking my view. "What is it, Rocco?"

When he finally turned around with this little fuzzy dog in his hands, my eyes immediately lit up.

Woof! It barked.

"Oh, my, God! You got me a puppy?" I squealed, racing over with my hands out.

"I shouldn't let yo bratty ass have it."

"C'mon, baby. I promise I'ma be good."

"Fuck being good. I wanna feel that pussy later," he sneered playfully before handing over the small, brown dog.

"Boy," I said and playfully rolled my eyes. "What breed is it?"

"She is a Shih Tzu."

"She's beautiful! Thank you, baby!" I squealed while throwing my arm around his neck. Rocco placed a kiss on my forehead.

"I figured you needed something to keep you company."

Before I could reply, there was a knock on the door.

"C'mon."

Santino peeked his head inside. "I see you got your gift."

"You knew about this?"

"Yeah. I told this fool you would like it."

"Wait a minute. How the hell did you get this dog here?"

Something about the situation still wasn't adding up for me.

"Look, I might as well tell ya. I brought you here to keep you out the way. In a few weeks, me and Santino plan to head back. We gotta get money and handle this nigga Vladir. I'on know how long we'll be gone. It could be a week, a month, maybe even six months. The dog was a gift to soften the blow."

"Really, Rocco! You brought me all the way out here, and you plan to leave?"

"It won't be forever. As soon as the business is handled, we'll talk about finding somewhere to settle down. I know you ain't happy to hear this, but I needed to keep you safe."

"I'ma go in here and call my shawty while y'all finish discussing this." Santino left the room and closed the door behind him.

"What if you don't ever make it back?" I asked Rocco the dreadful question.

"Then this will be your home for as long as you need it to be. My boy, who owns the place, lives out here with his wife. They've been instructed on what to do if I don't make it back. All you gotta do is let 'em know what you need, and they'll take care of it."

I wanted to cry so bad, but I knew that wouldn't help the situation. Rocco needed me to be strong, so that's what I planned to do.

"You're gonna make it back," I told him before putting a kiss on his lips.

Woof! The dog barked, and we both laughed.

Rocco

A week later...

"Baby, can I ask you a question?" Emera said.

"'Sup, shawty?"

We had just finished hitting a spliff and were now relaxing out on the patio. This past week had been hectic as fuck. Not only was a nigga's pockets hurting, but I couldn't make any moves. Being in a new city posed many problems. Cats weren't messing with us because we were from out of state. If we didn't come up with a quick solution, we would be forced to take drastic measures.

"Why don't you talk about your family?"

I glanced at Emera and let out a deep sigh. "Because it ain't shit to talk 'bout."

"What about your parents? Can you tell me how they passed?"

"Nah, that's dead, shawty."

She sucked her teeth and rolled her eyes. "I've told you

everything about myself, yet you're still a mystery to me. Why won't you trust me?"

As much as I loved her little ass, she was starting to work my nerves. Why couldn't she ever just leave well enough alone?

"I'll tell you in due time."

"C'mon, Rocco. I thought we weren't going to keep any more secrets."

"Damn, man! My pops was a dopehead who used me as a target for his rages when he couldn't get high. He killed my mama because she was fuckin' with some other nigga, and then his coward ass took his own life. Is that what you wanna know?"

Emera placed her hand over her mouth and gasped. "I'm so sorry, baby. I didn't mean to bring up any hurtful memories."

"I ain't sweating that shit. A nigga just don't like discussing the situation because it's irrelevant."

"So, who raised you?" she asked, and I shook my head.

"My mom's sister."

"That was a good thing. At least you had somebody to take you in."

"Nah, wasn't shit 'bout living with that bitch good. I went from one hellhole to another when she took me in. The only difference was that I was old enough to move around once I got sick of her shit."

"Well, as shitty as it was, at least you had a way out. I didn't even have that."

"Yeah, I guess. If that's what you wanna call it."

Emera climbed over the chair and straddled me. "I hope you know that I will never hurt you like they did," she claimed.

I stared into her eyes, searching for a sign of sincerity.

A big part of me felt that despite the way our story started, shawty actually had love for a nigga. The other part was still waiting for all this to backfire. If my punk-ass daddy hadn't taught me shit else, it was to never believe what you heard and only half of what you saw.

***

Three days later…

"There that nigga go right there." I pointed out the window.

For the past hour, me and Santino had been sitting outside of this small hole-in-the-wall club. A few days ago, we got info on a mark we could hit. Word around town was that the nigga was a big-time dope boy known for stunting and being flashy.

Since me and Santino had been limited on how we got our money, these dope boys were our only option. Hitting capers wasn't something I preferred to do, but a nigga couldn't just wait for some shit to magically pop off. I had to go out and get it by any means necessary.

When ol' boy hopped out of his 2020 Tesla Model X, I gripped my pistol in my right hand and opened the door with my left.

"Go around the back of the car just in case his ass tries to run." I instructed Santino.

"A'ight. I gotcha."

A few seconds later, I approached the nigga just before he made it to the door. "Yo, ain't your name Skootie?"

"Who wants to know?" he spat.

For a supposedly big-time dope dealer, I pictured this cat to look completely different. Skootie was about five-feet-six with a slim build and starter dreads. His head was small, like a tennis ball, and it didn't fit his body frame. Then the nigga was dressed basic as hell.

I pulled my pistol from behind my back and pointed it at him. "I wanna know."

"Ain't this about a bitch! I'm so sick of you young mufuckas that can't grind, so you go out and rob other hard workers. If you need to eat, I can teach ya, but this ain't the way, youngblood."

"Fuck out of here with that shit! You a damn drug dealer, nigga. How the hell you suddenly got morals? You poisonin' yo' community."

Skootie looked at me and snarled. "I'm not taking no losses," he uttered before he took off running.

Unfortunately for his ass, he didn't get that far. Santino was right there with his piece loaded and ready. All he needed was the word, and Skootie's brain would be on the front of his whip.

I eased up behind Skootie. "We can make this shit easy, or we can do it the hard way. It's yo' decision. But just so we clear, I'm getting what I came for. So it's in your best interest to comply and get this shit over with."

"Muthafucka!" He gritted while throwing his hands in the air.

"And oh yeah, only pussies put their hands on women. If you that fuckin' mad, get you some anger management!"

I swear if looks could kill, I would be a dead muthafucka. I pushed Skootie toward the driver's side of his car and forced him to get inside. Afterward, I ran around to the passenger side and hopped in.

"Take me to that money. And if you even think about doing something, your brains gon' be on that steering wheel."

He let out a deep breath.

***

An hour later, I pulled up to the QuikTrip on Main street. The person I was meeting was already parked in the back of the building. When she saw my whip, she hopped out and strutted over.

"You really came through. Thank you so much, Rocco! This money is the ticket I needed for me and Junior to start a new life," Summer cheerfully stated.

Summer was Skootie's baby mama. We met at this same store, not even a day after I touched down. I had just pulled up when I spotted shawty on the sidewalk crying her eyes out. Her nose was all bloody, and one eye was swollen shut. From what shawty told me, her and ol' boy had just gotten into a heated argument that turned into him beating her ass. To add insult to injury, the faggot put her out at the gas station.

I asked why she put up with that, and she told me it was because she didn't have the money to leave him. Now, usually, I didn't involve myself in domestic disputes, but she reminded me of Emera. They both wore that "I wanna be saved" look.

"It ain't no thang. I just hope you keep ya word. Leave this mufucka, and don't look back for shit."

"You don't have to worry about that. Once I get back into that truck, I'm leaving for good. It ain't nothing left here for me."

"Fa sho. Take care of yourself and lil' man."

"I will. And you take care of yourself as well. Hope everything works out with ol' girl. She's very lucky to have you." With that, Summer switched her fat ass back to the Yukon. As soon as shawty was inside, she sped away.

"Damn, lil' ma was stacked as hell. I can't believe you didn't try to hit that before she bounced." Santino grinned.

"Nah. Shawty was battling some serious demons. She didn't need me adding to her pain. Besides, I ain't even trying to play Emera like that."

"Nigga, you sure that's you in there?"

"Fuck is you talking about?"

"'Cause the old Rocco I knew didn't get in committed relationships, and he damn sho didn't turn down the chance to fuck a bad bitch."

"If you hadn't noticed, nigga, I got my own bad bitch at the crib. Now let's pull off. I'on like sitting up here like this."

Santino gave me a sly grin before pulling away. "I hear ya, playboy."

Emera

Two days later…

I tried my best to focus, but all the yelling from the other room had me completely distracted. Santino and his girl-friend, Novia, had been going at it for the past hour.

"I'm tired of this shit, Santino!" Novia spat.

"Well, leave then!" he shot back.

"Oh, I can leave. That ain't no problem!"

"Uh baby, just forget it. They killed my mood."

Rocco glanced up with my juices covering his beard and face. "Say, man, how the hell you focused on them while I'm doing this?"

"I'm sorry, baby. I swear it's not you. They are just getting on my nerves."

"So what. Let them do them while we do us."

Just then, we heard a loud thud as if something had been thrown into the wall. I eyed Rocco with a knowing look.

"This som' straight-up bullshit. These mufuckas been going at it like cats and dogs. Give me just a minute, baby. I'ma go holler at this fool."

"Please do 'cause a bitch can't even get a nut."

Rocco slid off the bed, laughing. He took the back of his hand and wiped his chin before stepping into a pair of shorts.

"I'll be back."

I laid there impatiently waiting for him to return. It seemed ever since Novia had shown up, everything had been chaotic. If she wasn't arguing with Santino, then she was complaining about something. Granted, this was a challenging situation for all of us. At the same time, she knew what she was getting into before bringing her ass out here.

Five minutes later, Rocco tipped back into the room, shaking his head. "What happened?"

"Man, I need to get him out of here quick before he fucks 'round and kill that girl."

"What she do?" I wanted to know.

"He ain't really say. All he told me is that he was 'bout to lay hands on her. Right now, I just need to let him blow off some steam."

"This is so messed up. How long y'all gonna be gone? You know I don't like being here with her by myself."

"We shouldn't be out for too long. I'll hit you up on the way back to see what you wanna eat."

"I swear it was so much more peaceful before she got here." I let out a long, frustrated breath.

"Yeah, I know. I'll hit you in a minute. Love you." Rocco put a kiss on my lips.

"Love you too," I told him.

***

Not even ten minutes after Rocco left, Novia was at our door, knocking.

"Wassup?" I asked, tying the robe around my waist.

Novia was standing there looking pitiful as hell. Her clothes were disheveled, her eyes were bloodshot red, and her hair was all over her head. I wouldn't say that Novia was ugly, but her makeup made quite a difference. She was about two inches taller than me with a dark-brown complexion, thick frame, and a big juicy booty.

"Can I talk to you for a minute?"

"About what?" I wasn't really in the mood to deal with her shenanigans.

"Can I please just come in for a minute? I'll make it quick."

Grabbing the door, I opened it wider for her to step inside.

"I know you probably think I'm the biggest bitch right now. It's a reason why I've been acting like this," she started to explain before I could even offer her a seat.

I looked at her with a blank expression.

"Please don't look at me like that."

"Look, I really don't know why you're coming to me. Ever since you've been here, we ain't said more than two words to each other. You always have an attitude about something, and even though it's not my business, I don't like how you've been treating Santino."

Novia rolled her eyes into her head and sucked her teeth. "Santino ain't as innocent as you think. That bastard made me abort my baby at three months pregnant. I pleaded for him to let me keep it. He said he wasn't ready for kids, and if I didn't get rid of it, then I was on my own. Even though I wanted my baby bad as hell, I couldn't picture letting Santino go. He was all I had.

"My mama had abandoned me when I was a teenager. I went to stay with my granny. She died not even six months after I got there. I was forced to go into a group home. Around that time, I met the guy I was with before I got with Santino. We were together for almost a year when he broke up with me.

"After giving him my heart and virginity, that muthafucka told me he wasn't looking for nothing serious. I was crushed for a long time until I met Santino. The first year and a half that we were rocking, shit was good between us. Then all of a sudden, everything just changed. He had bitches stepping to me left and right about them fucking. Even after I confronted Santino about the other women, he still wouldn't do right. He basically said that I had to deal with it since he was taking care of me. Over the years, the shit only got worse. It all started to take a real toll on my mental."

"If he's doing all that to you, why don't you just leave him?"

"I just told you that I don't have anybody else. Besides, I really love him. The thing is, I just can't let go of all the pain he's put me through. A big part of me still resents him for making me get an abortion."

"I'm really sorry to hear that you're going through all this. The best advice I can give you is to put yourself first. No matter how much you love someone, you can't make them do right by you. No amount of cursing and shouting will make him change if he's not ready to. Hell, you could be missing out on your soul mate by wasting time with him."

"Damn, I never looked at it like that." Novia put her head down as if she was processing it all.

When she finally glanced up, I noticed the tears in her eyes.

"Thank you, Emera. You don't know how much I needed to hear this. I guess I got a lot of thinking to do."

She leaned in, giving me a big hug. "Um, you're welcome," I mumbled, surprised by the sudden shift of her mood.

"So on another note, I got some liquor and edibles in the room. You down?"

I arched my brow while giving her the side look. *Why is she being nice all of a sudden?*

Rocco

At three o'clock in the morning, I stumbled back into the crib. Me and Santino rode around for a few hours before I dropped him off at this chick's house. I didn't think that was the right move to make, considering we had a price on our heads. Still, I kept my opinions to myself, not willing to babysit the next nigga's dick. Besides, my main focus was on getting my bread up, handling this nigga Vladir, and making sure my shawty was good. Anything beyond that was irrelevant.

All this back-and-forth bullshit that we'd been doing was weighing heavy on Emera. Even though she hadn't mentioned it, I could sense that she was still spooked. Any time there was a loud noise, shawty would damn near jump out of her skin. The shit was getting so bad that I could barely touch ma without her flinching. I needed to bust a move like yesterday.

"'Sup, shawty? What you doing up this late?" I asked Novia. She was standing in the kitchen, tossing back a bottle of water.

"Trying to sober up a little. Me and your girl stayed up all night getting fucked up, and now my head is pounding." She giggled.

"Oh yeah? Where she at now?"

"She passed out about an hour ago. So, where you boy at?" She tried to slide in.

"He hit a telly for the night to clear his head." Shawty thought she was slick, but I was slicker.

"Hmph. Tell me anything. I'm pretty sure he's with a bitch. It's cool, though." She shrugged.

I didn't know what she wanted me to say. It wasn't like I would throw my nigga under the bus.

"A'ight. Be cool, shawty. I'ma grab me a bottle of water and go pass out."

"Hol' up for a second, can I talk to you?" she asked, and I scratched the side of my head.

"Look, I ain't really trying to get in the middle of what y'all got going on."

"I think you gon' wanna hear this," she said and paused for a dramatic effect.

"What is it?"

"Um."

"Man, just spit that shit out."

"I think your girl and Santino got something going on."

"What? Hell nah! How you figure that shit?"

"Earlier when we were talking, she mentioned som' shit about how she didn't like the way I treated Santino. I was like, what that got to do with you? She gon' tell me that Santino is a good person. For a second, I thought maybe I was tripping, but then I noticed ol' girl got this beam in her eyes. The shit didn't sit right with me. And that's not it."

"One day, I caught Santino staring at Emera's ass. So you already know I checked him. He tried to make it seem like it was my imagination playing tricks on me. Stupidly, I fell for the bullshit until I caught him doing it again. That time when I confronted his ass, he didn't even try to deny it."

I stepped around Novia and headed for the refrigerator. After grabbing a bottle of water, I turned and made my way toward the door.

"Rocco, really! So you just gon' walk out?" She ran up to me and grabbed my arm.

"Fuck off of me! I'on know what type of shit you on right now, but I ain't with it. My girl ain't got nothin' to do with y'all bullshit."

"Your girl? Your girl? Nigga, I'm supposed to be your girl! How you gon' have that stripping bitch all in my face when you know I still love you? It's like you just don't give a damn about me. What about the fact that you left me when I needed you most, huh?" she cried.

I knew the time would come for me to have this conversation with shawty. A nigga just didn't think it would be now.

"Man, that shit is old with us. Fuck can I do about it now? We both with somebody else."

"I don't care about Santino. If you say that we can be together right now, I will break up with him. C'mon, Rocco. You know I'm still in love with you."

I was shocked to hear her admit that. We hadn't messed around since our teens, and even then, it wasn't that serious. Shawty was looking for the type of love her parents should have given her.

Being that I was young, a nigga wasn't capable of taking on such a significant role. So I set her free in hopes that she would find what she was looking for. I had no idea that someone would turn out to be my nigga.

When I found out she and Santino were dating, I let Santino know what the deal was. He didn't seem to trip since things hadn't been that deep with us. Until now, I thought everything was behind us, but I guess not. Novia tried to take my hand and put it on her butt. I quickly stepped away.

"Novia, it's obvious you drunk as hell. So I'ma let this shit slide. On some real shit, though, you need to go back there and sleep it off. If you keep fuckin' 'round, yo' feelings gon' get hurt."

"I'm not too drunk to understand what I'm saying. I love you, Rocco. Just please let me feel it again. I wanna take this pain away."

I was ready to respond when Novia grabbed the back of my head and smashed her lips into mine.

"What the fuck is going on?"

My neck swiveled toward the door, and that's when I saw Emera with tears streaming down her cheeks.

"So now I know who the guy is that broke your heart," she muttered while shooting daggers at Novia.

"What the fuck did you tell her?" I barked.

Novia stood there with a blank expression. "I didn't tell her shit."

"Quit lying, bitch! What the hell did you say?"

I was about to knock this broad's head off her shoulders.

"Rocco, this is not about what she said. It's about the fact you had this bitch in my face knowing that y'all had been together. Once again, you've managed to hurt me with your secrets. But you wanna talk about you can't trust me. Tuh! So does Santino know, or was I the only one in the dark?" She angrily swiped her tears away. "You know what, it doesn't even matter.

Since you wanted him so bad, you can have his ass."

When Emera stomped away, I was right behind her.

"Hol' up, ma."

"Stay the hell away from me!" she screamed, slamming the door in my face.

"Fuck!" I gritted.

***

"Your room is paid up for a week. Get the fuck out!" I belted after coming to an abrupt stop.

I woke up at the crack of dawn to get this bitch Novia the hell away from us. Santino wasn't answering his phone, so I took it upon myself to handle the situation. I didn't even offer an explanation as to where I was taking her. I just drove straight over here to the Extended Stay.

"What am I supposed to do after that?" she had the nerve to question.

"That ain't my problem. You better hit Santino up."

"Okay, and what about money? I need food to eat."

I threw the car in park and reached inside my pocket. After peeling off two twenties, I slammed them on the console.

"Take that shit and get the fuck out of my whip!" I piped.

Novia sucked her teeth. "Listen, Rocco, I didn't mean—"

"Aye… Aye, save that shit. I ain't even trying to hear it."

She grabbed the money and hopped out. Before she could even close the door, I peeled off on her ass.

On my way back to the crib, I hit Santino's line for the fifth time. That fool still didn't answer.

"Where the hell this nigga at?" I mumbled aloud.

It wasn't like him not to answer my calls. *I need to do a pop-up at ol' girl's crib and find out what's going on.*

Twenty minutes later, I was outside of shawty's door where I'd been knocking for the longest.

"Hey, are you looking for Jamila?" A young, light-skin, chubby girl with a baby face moseyed out of the apartment next door.

I ran my hand over my head. "Who dat?"

She squinted her eyes. "The girl who lives here."

"Damn. I didn't know what shawty's name was. But anyway, I'm looking for my nigga. He had me drop him off here last night."

"Well, I haven't seen her today. She's usually at work around this time, but I see her car is still parked. She must really like your boy 'cause she don't miss work for nobody," she said and giggled.

All of a sudden, I got this strange feeling. Even when Santino was laid up, he made it his business to check in. Something about this scene wasn't right.

"Say, do me a favor," I asked ol' girl.

"Wassup?"

"Check that door for me."

"Hell nah! What if I walk in on them fuckin' or something?"

"Look, my boy is expecting me. We supposed to go handle something important, but he ain't answering his phone. I feel like som' ain't right."

She sighed and bit down on her bottom lip. "Now that

you mention it, this does seem strange. Like I said, Jamila, don't miss work for nobody."

"So check that out for me."

Shawty switched over to the door and put her hand on the knob. "I doubt the door is unlocked, but I'll see."

With little force, the door popped open.

"That's weird. Why would she have her door unlocked? Jamila? Jamila? Some guy out here looking for his friend. Are you decent in there?" she called out.

Silence.

I stepped over to the door and tried to go inside.

"Hol' up. You can't go in here."

"Why not?"

"'Cause I'on know you. Hell, you could be somebody crazy she was dealing with. I'll go check it out." She eased into the apartment while still calling out to Jamila.

I stayed outside by the door and waited for her to return.

"Noooo!" I suddenly heard her scream. Shawty shot out of the apartment like that bitch
was on fire.

"Waddup?"

"They're... They're dead. Somebody killed them. It's so much blood. Oh, my God!" she rambled.

I pushed her out the way and rushed inside the apartment. "Ah, fuck!" I uttered.

Santino and the chick were facedown in the hall with gunshots in the back of their heads. Judging by the way their bodies were sprawled out, it looked as if they'd tried to run.

I backpedaled out the door.

"Are they really dead?" the broad asked, and I nodded.

She was squatted by the door balling her eyes out.

"Ye-Yeah, they dead," I stammered.

"Wait, where are you going? We need to call the police."

That broad was crazy as hell to think I would stick around. A black man plus a crime scene equaled an automatic lockup.

As I ran over to my whip, I could still hear her yelling at me. I hopped inside and quickly peeled off. By the time I made it home, I was drenched in sweat. My shirt was literally soaked and wet. I snatched it over my head and tossed it in the back seat before getting out.

"Yo, Emera. We gotta go, ma," I called out to her.

Emera came strutting into the room with an attitude. My eyes went to the red duffle bag before they traveled to the old lady behind her. It was the same woman that was with her moms at the restaurant.

"What the hell is going on here?"

"I called Ms. London to come get me after everything went down last night. We are done, Rocco. You've hurt me to the core, and I can't do this with you. It's best if we part ways now before it's too hard for me to walk away."

I released a deep breath. "Now ain't the time for this. Som' shit popped off, and we need to bounce."

"I'm not going. Ms. London is going to take me with her."

"Fuck is you talking about? I'm not 'bout to let you out my sight."

"How are you going to make me stay?" Emera spat while throwing her hand on her hip.

I marched over to Emera and grabbed her by the arm.

"Let go of me," she hissed.

"Listen, Rocco, holding Emera against her will is not the answer. She'll only resent you in the end. Just give her time to cool off and see how everything goes from there."

"No offense, ma'am, but I ain't letting her leave with you. Emera, bring yo' ass on right now," I spat.

I wasn't playing games with shawty any more. She could be mad all she wanted, just as long as she got her ass in the damn car. All of a sudden, the old lady pulled a gun from her purse.

"What the hell!" *I know she don't plan on shooting me.*

"Nah, she ain't going nowhere with you. So I'ma need you to back the fuck up!"

I was shocked when her old, church-lady ass pointed the gun at my dome.

"Ms. London, where did you get that gun from, and why do you have it?" Emera questioned.

Ms. London's phone started ringing. She used her free hand to remove it from her purse. With the Glock still trained on me, she spoke into her cell.

"Hello! Yes, I have them both right here. Okay. I'll be waiting." She ended the call and slid her phone back inside her purse. "I'm sorry, Emera. I love you like a daughter, but that price on your head was too big for me to turn it down."

Ain't this about a bitch!

Emera was standing there shooting daggers at Ms. London. "Wow! You supposed to belong to the Lord. Why are you doing this?" Emera barked.

"Oh, honey, that ain't got nothing to do with it. I still love the Lord, but I need this money. My son don' let my house go into foreclosure, my utilities are behind, and I barely have food. The way I see it, the Lord used you as a way for me to get this money. Besides, your mama owes me. Anytime I tried to get off drugs, it was her that kept me down. She was always coming around, telling me to take one more hit. Hell, it's her fault I started in the first place. So yeah, y'all owe me this money."

Emera glanced at me and then back at Ms. London. Before I could blink, shawty had football-tackled the shit out of Ms. London.

"Owww!" Ms. London howled as she hit the floor with a hard thud.

She grabbed Emera's leg, causing her to crash right beside her. They started tussling.

I ran over, trying to break it up.

Pow!

"Oh shit, shawty!" I mumbled when Emera's eyes closed. Using my foot, I pushed Ms. London over to the side. Noticing the blood leaking from her body, a nigga breathed a sigh of relief.

I thought my shawty had been hit.

"Look what you made me do! I didn't wanna do this! Oh, Lord, what did I do?" Emera rambled as I pulled her up.

I grabbed shawty and buried her head in my chest to prevent her from seeing the lady take her last breath.

"You can't blame yourself for this. It was either you or her. Not to sound insensitive, but we gotta go."

"What if she's not dead. We can probably save her."

"She gone, ma. We gotta go."

Emera was still crying when I pulled her out the door.

Emera

Ten minutes later…

"Can I trust you to stay put while I go pay for this gas?" Rocco questioned with a serious look.

"Where the hell am I gonna go?" I spat, and he smirked.

When Rocco finally got out, I threw my head inside my hands. I still couldn't believe that Ms. London had tried to set us up. We'd been in contact for weeks, and she hadn't mentioned anything. All she'd seem to care about was my safety. She didn't even inquire about my location or if I was with anyone. I guess she was aware that asking specific details would trigger my suspicions. Therefore, she waited patiently until I revealed the information voluntarily.

The shit was so messed up. Santino was dead, Vladir was still after us, and now, I was a murderer.

"A fucking murderer!" I cried.

At that moment, I felt sick to my stomach, like I was going to throw up. Just as I rolled the window down to get some fresh air, I heard a loud scream.

"Ahhh!"

I glanced to my left and saw a white man dressed in all black. He was headed this way with a gun. *Oh shit!* My eyes widened in shock. *This gotta be somebody with Vladir. I told Rocco we should wait before stopping to get gas.*

Frantically, I reached under the seat for his gun. When I realized it wasn't there, I knew I was fucked. My eyes landed back on the man, and it seemed like he was looking right at me. I was scared shitless.

"Get down!" the door flew opened, and Rocco yelled at me.

I quickly laid down and covered my head. "Ahhhhhh!" I screamed when bullets started flying through the back window.

Callie was barking in her cage, so I leaned up to check on her. I had eased up when a bullet whizzed past my head.

"Oh shit!" I uttered while ducking back down.

"Stay down!" Rocco yelled as he fired off shots at the other dude.

The gunfire lasted about a minute before it finally came to an abrupt halt. That's when Rocco hopped back in the car and peeled off. I kept my ass right there on the floor until he told me it was safe to get up. When I looked in the back and saw that Callie was safe, I breathed a sigh of relief.

We were going about a hundred miles per hour as Rocco whipped his car in and out of traffic.

"I'ma be sick," I mumbled and leaned onto the door.

"Hol' on, shawty. These mufuckas behind us. I can't stop until I lose them."

"I can't hold it," I groaned and wiped the sweat beads from my forehead.

"Grab that plastic bag from the back. Dump the stuff out and use that."

"Ugh!" I groaned while sticking my head inside the bag.

The vomit was spewing out of my mouth like a faucet. By the time we finally made it to the expressway, I'd thrown up three times. Rocco had me toss the bag out of the window.

"Are they still behind us?" I questioned as I leaned my head against the seat.

"I think they gone. I haven't seen 'em for a minute. You good?"

"Not really. I still feel nauseous. Was that somebody working for Vladir?"

"It had to be. We ain't got nobody else gunning for us."

"Rocco, what are we going to do? We can't run forever." I finally opened my eyes and looked at him.

"I promise I'ma handle this shit once and for all. Just let me get you somewhere safe, a'ight?"

Although Rocco said he would handle it, I just didn't know. Vladir wasn't showing any signs of stopping until we were dead.

***

"Shawty, you good in there?" I heard Rocco call to me.

I glanced down at the pregnancy test in my hand and released a deep breath. "Shit! How the hell did I let this happen?"

Me and Rocco ain't in no position to raise a child right now. It's too much going on. Besides, we just got together. Having a baby this soon in the relationship can complicate things. I wasn't even sure if Rocco wanted kids. There was just a lot to think about before I made a decision. After flushing the toilet, I slid the test in my pocket and washed my hands.

We had arrived in Chicago a little over two hours ago. After riding around for a while trying to find a place, Rocco finally settled on the Embassy Suites downtown. We only had plans to stay for the night because Rocco wanted me to be somewhere more secluded.

"Come sit down so we can eat," Rocco instructed when I emerged from the bathroom.

I went over to the table and sat across from Rocco. "Baby, this is so sweet. Where did you find this stuff?"

Even with all the bullshit going on, he'd managed to attempt a romantic setup. There was a vase with two red, long-stemmed roses, a few small candles, and a bottle of wine that was chilling on ice in the middle of the small table.

I love this man so much!

"I went to the store while you were in the shower," he replied.

"Wow! That was fast."

"Nah, it wasn't fast. You were just in there a long ass time."

I let out a little giggle.

"Thank you! This was really thoughtful, especially with all that we have going on."

"Go ahead and eat. You need to put something on your stomach."

I picked up a slice of pizza and put it to my mouth. When the smell hit my nostrils, it took everything in me not to gag. I didn't want to ruin Rocco's surprise, but I couldn't eat this pizza.

"What's wrong with you?" Rocco queried.

"My stomach still feels a little weird from earlier." *Please don't let him suspect anything.*

Rocco eyed me for a minute before finally nodding. "You ain't drinking either?"

"Um. It's sweet, so it'll probably upset my stomach too," I said, and he stared at me
blankly. "I'm sorry, baby. You did really good. It's just that my stomach has been acting weird."

"It's all good, ma. We both had a long ass day. Let's get some rest and start over tomorrow."

"Okay." I half-smiled.

Rocco blew out the candles as I eased over to the bed.

"Say, that dog ain't sleeping with us."

"Please? Just for tonight? She's probably still shaken up." I poked out my bottom lip as I held Callie in my arms.

Scratching his neck, he glared at me. "A'ight, man, but just for tonight. But she ain't sleeping in the middle."

Rocco and I got comfortable in the bed. Throwing an arm around my waist, he snuggled up behind me.

"This is going to be over soon, right?" I asked.

Rocco didn't verbally reply, but the kiss he put on my neck spoke volumes. That was his way of saying he couldn't make any promises about our future.

A single tear slipped from my eye as I drifted off.

Rocco

A few days later…

"**D**amn, nigga, we ain't seen you around in a minute. When you get back?" this cat named Buzz questioned.

After making sure Emera was tucked away safely, I made the long drive back to Oklahoma. The first thing I did was pay my condolences to Santino's people. I hit them off with some ends to help cover the expenses of his funeral. I figured that was the least I could do. Once I took care of that business, I went and hollered at my homeboy who had them choppers. He hooked me up with two Glocks, an Uzi, and some ammo.

Trekking up, I smashed Buzz in the face with the butt of my pistol. His shit split on impact, causing blood to gush out.

"What the fuck, nigga?" he yelped.

"Where that muthafucka Vladir at?"

"Fuck am I supposed to know?" Buzz snapped while holding his nose.

"I guess you think I'm stupid. Nigga, I know you were in that car the other day."

"What car?"

I fired off a shot into Buzz's kneecap. His ass started hollering like a bitch.

"Where is Vladir!"

"I swear I'on know! He told me, uh... Shit! My muthafuckin' knee burning!"

I pulled back on the trigger. "Keep talking before I make the other one burn!"

"The last time we talked, he told me that he was going to look for you."

"Call that nigga up now."

Buzz took out his phone and dialed Vladir. He answered after a few rings. "Put it on speaker."

"What is it, Buzz? I'm kinda in the middle of something."

"Say, bitch, meet me at the Buck Thomas Park in half an hour."

"Who is this?"

"You know who I am, nigga! Quit playing games."

"Rocco, it's so good to hear from you." Vladir chuckled.

"Fuck these head games. You gon' meet up with me or what?"

"Under one condition."

"What's that?"

"Be prepared to die 'cause you won't be walking away."

I raised my pistol and shot Buzz in the face.

"Don't count on it ol' hoe ass nigga!"

After tossing the cell into a nearby drain, I went back to

my whip and hopped inside.

When I finally made it to the park twenty minutes later, I noticed a white van near the baseball field. Instinctively, I reached for my pistol and set it on my lap. While easing past the vehicle, I tried my best to peep inside. Unfortunately, the tint was too dark for me to see.

Scurrrr!

"Shit," I grumbled as I jammed on my brakes.

"Hey, what the hell is your problem? You almost ran us over!" It was a white guy with what looked to be his wife and teenage sons.

"My bad," I said, throwing up a hand.

"Idiot!" one of them called out as they hurried to the van.

This shit got me bugging.

"Where this nigga at?" I mumbled.

That van was the only vehicle on the lot. So that meant Vladir wasn't here.
Just as I pulled into a parking spot, my cell started going off. I snatched it up.

"I'm here, muthafucka. Where you at?"

"Rocco, I'm so disappointed. It seems ever since you've fallen in love, all your common sense has gone out the window."

"Fuck is you talking about?"

"Did you honestly think I would meet you there? C'mon. That would have been too easy."

"So, you scared now?" I asked.

"You know me. I've never been scared of anything. It's just that tonight, I've decided to switch it up a bit. The whole cat-and-mouse chase has gotten old. I'd much rather go be with that pretty little thing of yours than to play street soldiers with you."

"Nice try, nigga, but you don't know where she's at."

"Once again, you've underestimated me. While you were focused on dodging my decoy in Kansas, you failed to see me swoop right in. I was able to follow y'all all the way to the Windy City without you knowing. And now that I know you're there, I can go sample that pussy without interruptions."

"I swear on everything I love, I will body yo' ass if you go anywhere near her!" I exploded.

"Ha-ha! You'll first have to make it out of your situation," he said and ended the call.

I was ready to call him back when the sounds of tires screeching caught my attention. My eyes shot up, and that's when I saw the white van. The two teenage boys hopped out, followed by the fake ass mom and dad.

Fuck!

Emera

ver since Rocco left, I'd been bored out of my damn mind. I was taking Callie on walks every hour just to keep myself occupied. While she seemed to enjoy the outings, I was about to go bat shit crazy. All I kept thinking about was Rocco and if he was safe. I told myself I wouldn't call unless it was vital.

Honestly, I was just missing my mama and Kitty like crazy. If only I could go back in time, I would do so many things differently.

Ring! Ring! My cell going off brought me from my thoughts. When I saw it was Rocco, my heart pumped vigorously.

"Wassup, baby?" I answered.

"Yo, shawty," he said, and then the line suddenly went silent.

"Hello, Rocco? Rocco? Shit," I hissed.

My phone had just died. I hopped up and trekked into the bedroom. Just as I grabbed the charger, I heard Callie barking.

"Shut up, Callie! You gettin' on my nerves now. Shit!" I shouted.

With the charger in my hand, I tipped back into the living room. Callie was by the closet door, still yapping. I told her to shut up again, but she wouldn't listen.

"What's wrong with you?"

Barrrrrr-arrrrrr!

"Callie, what's yo' damn pr—"

The door suddenly flew open, knocking Callie halfway across the room.

"Ahhh!"

I took off running, but Vladir was right behind me. He grabbed me by the hair and yanked me back.

"Where you think you going? Huh, bitch? I bet you and Rocco thought I wouldn't catch up to you. Looks like the joke on y'all."

Callie ran over and bit Vladir on the ankle.

"Get off me, you little rat!"

Pow!

My heart broke in half when Vladir pulled out a gun and shot my baby.

"Noooooo!" I wailed.

At that point, I was kicking and screaming. Snot was running into my mouth, but I didn't give a damn. Callie was my heart, and it hurt to know that he'd killed her.

Once Vladir took me into the room, he tossed me on the bed.

"First, we gonna have some fun, and then I'ma kill you," he threatened.

"No. Please don't do this," I cried.

Vladir trudged over and slapped the shit out of me.

"Mmm," I groaned as the taste of blood filled my mouth.

He'd popped me so hard that my teeth cut through my lip.

"I'm done playing games! Either get undressed or take a bullet in yo' head."

Hurriedly, I stripped out of my clothes until I was down to my bra and panties. Vladir's ol' creepy-ass came over stroking himself.

"That body is so sexy, and I bet that pussy is super tight. It gotta be good for Rocco to lose his mind as he did. Yeah, I'ma have a lot of fun with you."

"You are sick! I know about what you did to my mama!" I spat.

"So now it's not a secret!" he spat, dropping his pants. My eyes widened. *What the fuck!*

"Don't look so alarmed. This is just a result of you and your buddies," he stated menacingly.

Vladir had some type of bag that was strapped to his stomach, and his penis was just hanging there looking like Snuffleupagus. It was scary.

"This here is an ostomy bag. When your lil' friend shot me, the bullet damaged my colon. Now, I'm forced to walk around with it for life. Also, I suffer from permanent erectile dysfunction. In case your pea brain doesn't know what that is, it means I can't get a hard-on. So although we won't be able to have sex, there are other things we can do."

"Vladir... I'm sooo—"

"Shut the fuck up! I don't wanna hear shit from you. Matter of fact, get ready to suck my dick!"

"What?"

"You heard me. I want you to suck it real good."

"But you just said that you can't get it up." I was so confused.

"That has nothing to do with the feeling. Now, shut the hell up like I told you and put it in your mouth!" He roughly grabbed the back of my head.

As soon as his nasty dick hit my tongue, I had to fight the urge to vomit. Not only did it taste sour, but it was also covered in gray, prickly hairs. On top of that, I couldn't get the visual of that bag out of my head. It was taking everything in me not to throw up all over him.

"Yeah… Just like that. I see you're a real pro with that tongue. It's even better than your mother's."

With a scowl on my face, I glanced up just in time to see Vladir with his eyes closed. *Muthafucka!*

I slid my hand from under the pillow and stabbed the needle into his leg. As quickly as I could, I injected the liquid. His eyes popped open.

"Arrrrrgh! You stupid whore!" He smashed me in the face with the butt of his pistol.

"Uh!" My neck snapped back.

"You are dead?" he roared while snatching the needle out of his leg.

Shit! It didn't work. What the fuck happened? My eyebrows raised in confusion.

Vladir pointed the gun at me. Knowing this was the moment I would die, all I could do was squeeze my eyes shut. Suddenly, I heard a loud noise.

Bump!

I peeked one eye open and noticed Vladir down on the floor with his body stiff as a board.

"What. what. did you do to me?" he slurred almost inaudibly.

Once I realized what was happening, I leaped from the bed and grabbed the gun. Vladir tried to put up a fight, but it was useless. The gram and a half of heroin now floating through his system had deemed him momentarily paralyzed.

"I just made you an addict. Now you'll get the chance to walk in my mama's shoes. Oh yeah, the joke is on you, bitch!"

Epilogue

One year later...

Waaaaa! Waaaaa!

"**M**an, I swear she be doing that shit on purpose," Rocco grumbled as he pulled out of me.

We were trying to get in a little quickie before Baby Girl got up, but I guess she had other plans for us. I giggled.

"Yeah, her little butt be blocking hard. You want me to get her?" When I tried to sit up, Rocco pushed me back on the bed.

"Nah, you stay just like that. I'm getting my nut this time," he fussed, and I shook my head.

After throwing on a pair of boxers, Rocco shuffled out of the room. *Now he knows damn well that we ain't gon' finish.*

Our two-month-old daughter, Harlee, was known for casting spells. I swear, as soon as you laid eyes on her, you'd instantly become putty in her hands. This was mostly true of Rocco, as he never seemed to get enough of her. He would often sit up all night in the rocking chair with her laid on his chest. So if anybody was to blame for her being spoiled, it was his ass.

After twenty minutes went by and Rocco still hadn't returned, I got up and threw on a nightgown. Tipping down the hall to Harlee's nursery, I found Rocco in his favorite spot.

"Mhm. I thought you were coming back?"

Rocco glanced up at me with a sly grin. "You know how this shit is. When she put that magic on a nigga, it be over from there."

I gazed at them with a loving smile. Harlee looked like me and Rocco combined as one person. She had my skin tone, high cheekbones, and hair with Rocco's full lips, light brown eyes, and slender nose. If I'd ever done anything right in my life, it was making that perfect angel.

"You sad, man. This why she be acting like that. She knows you gonna fall for it."

"Damn right! Daddy gonna be there any time she needs me. Ain't that right, ma?"

Harlee grinned as if she understood what her daddy was saying.

"I'm going to take a shower. If you get the strength to put her down, you know where to find me."

I switched out and went back to our room. Once in the shower, I lathered my entire body. The water was feeling good, so I stood underneath it for a while. By the time I was ready to wash again, Rocco was climbing in behind me.

"I see she let you slip away."

"Just for a minute." He winked and picked me up.

After pushing himself inside of me, he started to rock gently. I wrapped my arms around his neck and circled my hips.

Rocco stuck his tongue in my mouth and kissed me passionately.

"Mmm," I moaned.

No matter how many times we had sex, I couldn't get enough of this man. Each time was like a new experience, and I was never left unsatisfied.

After Rocco and I finished having sex, we cleaned up and dressed for the day. I went and peeked in on Harlee while he smoked a blunt.

"She still asleep?" Rocco asked when I finally joined him on the balcony. He passed me the blunt.

"Knocked out cold. What you do to my baby? She never sleeps for more than twenty minutes." I hit the blunt a couple of times before passing it back to Rocco.

"We had a little talk. I told her she needed to chill because mama be getting jealous when she don't get her time."

"Boy, you play so damn much. Don't be telling my baby that." Rocco put his arm around my waist.

"You do be getting jealous. It's all good, though. Daddy gonna make sure his girl gets her time from now on." When he put a kiss on my neck, my body shivered.

"I love it out here. It's so peaceful." I inhaled deeply to take in some fresh air.

Rocco and I had decided that the best move for our family was to stay in Chicago. We didn't want Harlee to have any connections to our past life. With the help of our realtor, we found a foreclosed house in Glenview for a killer price. The house was huge. Not only did it sit on ten acres of land, but it also had over twenty rooms, ten bathrooms, and a six-car garage.

We used the extra money left from the purchase to have

everything remodeled. Our house now had a movie theater, two living rooms, a sauna, and a workout room. My favorite part of the house was the champagne room where I did my private dances for Rocco.

Ten minutes later, Rocco and I walked into our barn. "You got the baby monitor turned up, right?"

"Yes, baby. It's turned up."

"A'ight, cool. Wake up, nigga," Rocco said, slapping Vladir's face.

His eyes popped open as he wildly stared at us.

"I need my fix right now. I'm starting to get sick. It's been two days." As soon as he said that, vomit spewed from his mouth.

We jumped back to keep the throw up from splattering on us.

"Nasty muthafucka!" Rocco belted. "Is this what you want, huh?" Rocco dangled the needle in front of Vladir like a carrot.

"C'mon. I'm feening here, man. Uhhh," Vladir groaned while doubling over.

"Maybe next time, you'll think before you try to bite my wife."

"Baby, you think I should give it to him?"

I glared at Vladir and rolled my eyes. "Yeah. Go ahead."

Vladir was now a full-blown junkie. True to my word, I was making sure he had a life similar to the one he'd forced on my mama.

A while back, Rocco confesse the secret he'd been hiding was that Vladir was the one who got my mama hooked on drugs.

What I didn't know is that they dated before I was born. Apparently, Vladir was crazy as hell back then. He was really possessive when it came to Mama, so she decided to leave him. When Vladir found out about her plans, he injected her with Heroin. That led to Mama down a long road of self-destruction.

Once Rocco finally told me the truth, we devised a plan to handle Vladir once and for all. See, to go up against a crazed man like Vladir, we had to be able to think like him. Right before Rocco left town, we'd set up heroin filled syringes all over the house. We'd also hidden guns in inconspicuous places just in case I couldn't reach a needle. Some may say that what we did was risky as hell. We were aware of the consequences, but what were the alternatives? Vladir was never going to stop. He'd already killed my mama, Callie, and Santino.

The silver lining in all of this was that Rocco and I were now billionaires. With Vladir under our control, we were able to take over all his money and assets. In exchange, we provided him with the necessary essentials and his daily fixes. To this day, we still weren't sure of what he did for a living. All we knew is that whatever it was, he'd generated a lot of money doing it.

***

The next morning, I left Rocco and Harlee sleeping in our bedroom while I went to the home gym. After doing a forty-five-minute Zumba workout, I went for a three-mile run. During my pregnancy, a bitch had gained over seventy-five pounds. I was now trying to get my body back in shape.

Just as I neared our home, I slowed my run to a light jog when I noticed a dark-blue car sitting out front of our house. *Who the hell is that?* Nobody lived within a mile radius of us. The only time a vehicle drove this way was to turn around. *Maybe it's somebody that's lost.* I approached the sedan and knocked on the dark tinted window.

"Excuse me, are you lost?" I asked, but nobody answered. "Hello!" I knocked again.

When the window finally rolled down, I was shocked to see the person sitting behind it.

"What are you doing here?" I gritted.

"I came to get some things off my chest."

"Are you crazy? How did you even find me, Nolen?"

He looked like a completely different person with his long hair, scraggly beard, and shallow eyes. Something about this felt strange.

"You'd be surprised at how easy it was to hunt you down."

Within a blink of an eye, he reached out the window and pointed a gun at me.

"Huh!" I gasped, stumbling backward. "Wh… W… What are you doing?" I finally managed to get out.

"Let me paint a quick picture for you, Emera. Over a year ago, my father reached out. He said it was important for us to meet. Confused as to why he'd chosen then to contact me, I blew him off. However, once we broke up, I decided it was time to face him. During our first dinner, he shared an interesting story. Apparently, before you started stripping, you were robbing," he said and paused.

My eyes widened, and my mouth fell wide open. *Wait? Vladir is Nolen's father? What the hell!*

"I see it's starting to click for you. Well, hold on, because I got a little more. Before Vladir disappeared, he told me that y'all were behind everything. Initially, I didn't believe his story, then it hit me. You were the same person who lied, schemed, and cheated. Why wouldn't it be possible for you to do all those other things? After Vladir went missing, I knew just who to look for."

"Nol—"

"Shut up! I'm done listening to your lies. It's time for you to pay for your sins. For years, I waited to meet my father, only to have him taken away by you. Now, your daughter will know this same pain. By the way, she's beautiful. Hopefully, she won't turn out like her whore of a mother."

"Nolen, please don't kill me!"

He let out a maniacal chuckle. "Don't worry, I ain't gon' kill you. Can't say the same for your man, though."

Suddenly, my eyes widened as thoughts of Rocco went through my head. Spinning on my heels, I turned towards the door. "What did you do?" I screamed.

Rocco was sprawled out in the doorway. He wasn't moving, and blood was everywhere.

"Roccoooo!"

"Have a nice life, Emera," Nolen called out just as I made it to Rocco.

Kneeling next to him, I gently lifted his head into my lap. Scanning my eyes over his body, I noticed the small bullet hole in his neck and the one in his chest.

"Nooooo! Somebody, help me please. Rocco, baby, get up!"

His eyes fluttered as a gurgling sound escaped his lips. "I... love..."

He was trying to tell me that he loved me when his body suddenly went limp.

"Oh, my, God! Oh, my, God! Wait, Nolen, help me please!

Vladir is not dead…" My words trailed off as I watched his car disappear out of sight.

"I'm going to get you some help, Rocco. Please don't die on me," I cried.

"Yo, shawty, wake up! You having another nightmare."

"Huh! What?"

My eyes popped open. Glancing around, I noticed that Rocco and I were still in the bed. Sweat was pouring all over, and my face was covered in tears. I wiped them away as my eyes settled on Rocco.

"Baby!" I exclaimed, tugging at his clothes to examine his body.

"Yo, shawty, chill. I'm good. You were just dreaming." He chuckled, pulling me into him.

"I'on know, baby. That shit felt too damn real."

I could vividly see Nolen's face with that menacing look.

"What did you dream?" he questioned.

I told Rocco about the nightmare, and once I was finished, he had this blank expression.

"What? What's the matter?"

Rocco reached into the nightstand and handed me a piece of paper.

"What's this?"

"I didn't wanna tell ya this 'cause I ain't want you stressing, but this was in the mailbox the other day."

Staring down at the paper, I silently read the words.

I'm coming for you

The words were written in bold, red ink. My eyes shot up

to Rocco. "You don't think…"

Before I could get my sentence out, there was a loud thud downstairs. Rocco and I glanced at each other.

The End

I hope you enjoyed reading this novella. If you will, please leave a review. All feedback is welcomed!

Other reads by the author
Blurred Lines (2 book series)

Ways to stay in touch with the author-
Facebook N.L. Hudson/ Like Page (notifications)
*I have a reader's group, but it's not active. (For the love of books) I've started a new group called N.L. Hudson Book Thuggin. If you like to join that one, just send a request, and I'll accept it. Please allow patience with group interaction, as it is a brand new group.
Instagram- authoress_nlhudson
Twitter- @NLHudson3
Email- authoressnlhudson@yahoo.com